Memories Will Always Linger
A Novel History

by
Elizabeth Tidwell

1663 LIBERTY DRIVE, SUITE 200
BLOOMINGTON, INDIANA 47403
(800) 839-8640
WWW.AUTHORHOUSE.COM

Memories Will Always Linger is a post-Civil War history of Eastern Augusta County, Virginia, undergirding a lost object mystery. Many historical figures are mentioned, including Basic City's founders, Langhorne family members, and administrators of the Brandon Institute and Fairfax Hall. Actual names are used, although their words and activities are fictionalized. Most other characters are composite. Every effort has been made, through extensive research and interviews, to give an accurate representation of the life and times of the site and region.

© 2005 Elizabeth Tidwell. All Rights Reserved.

No part of this book may be reproduced, stored in a retrieval system, or transmitted by any means without the written permission of the author.

First published by AuthorHouse 06/06/05

ISBN: 1-4208-4786-4 (sc)

Printed in the United States of America
Bloomington, Indiana

This book is printed on acid-free paper.

This book is dedicated to
all those who have
lived and written
the history
of Fairfax Hall
and its environs.

Acknowledgements

My sincerest thanks to

Karen Vest, archivist at the Waynesboro Public Library, for so much help negotiating the local history files, introducing new resources, and endless encouragement.

Readers of the final manuscript—Karen Vest and Candy Cassell.
   Surely any remaining errors are my own.
Of an earlier version—my mother, Frances McMains; my aunt,
   Norma Fairey, and Mark Kearney of the Waynesboro Book 'em event.
My colleagues from the University of Virginia Health System
   Development Office who spent lunch hours reading dialogs
   aloud so I could listen for authenticity,

Fairfax Hall Alumnae from Amelia Court House, Virginia to Australia, who shared their memories and impressions. It would have been mere history without you.

To past and present site administrators and owners who shared their knowledge and access.

To neighbors and friends who shared my own Fairfax Hall living experience.

To many family members, friends, colleagues, and new acquaintances who encouraged me along the way.

Chapter 1

She decided to lease the apartment the day of the flood. Not that the rising water would reach her current home. It is over two miles from the normally placid river, hardly more than a stream. However, the sight of a temporary lake encroaching on two gas stations only blocks down the nearby street added a final—if somewhat silly—reason for the move.

Three rooms in the old building on the city's eastern high ground now held additional appeal. Her second visit to the site—with measuring tape this morning—confirmed that her few pieces of furniture, three racks of clothes and mounds of boxes would fit. Just barely. The newspaper advertisement read, "Unique one-bedroom apartment for rent. All utilities paid. . . ."

A first-viewing three days before revealed the one-of-a-kind location, a dorm mother's apartment in an old girls' school. Today's measurements primed sketchy plans for living arrangements. Room 216A, twelve by fourteen feet, would serve as a combination living room and kitchen. Room 216-B, fifteen by nineteen feet, would be a bedroom and office. The small bath between sported a claw foot bathtub with improvised shower hardware and curtain ring, toilet, and small sink. No room for more.

As possible room arrangements flowed through her brain, Adelia descended the grand staircase, crossed the wood-paneled lobby and the porte-cochere, climbed into her aging Toyota, and threw her notes on the passenger seat next to the empty Diet Dr Pepper bottle. Driving down the second half of the long, semi-circular driveway, she passed the winter-brown front-yard pasture where large patches of snow still lingered. She quickly planned a route of main roads for the two-and-a-half mile trip downtown to pick up mail. Heavy rains that morning guaranteed spot flooding in the neighborhood's low-lying back streets Adelia often traveled to avoid traffic delays at the railroad bridge construction site.

Her first Waynesboro home is less than half a mile from the new place—down the hill and over another bridge of the same railroad, into the several streets dotted mostly by one-family homes, small business enterprises, and the quadplex. The quad is an old house divided into four units where she has lived in the upper-east-side, one-bedroom apartment for seventeen months. The greater neighborhood also includes a lumberyard, an elementary school, and a string of apartment complexes about halfway between Adelia's two locations.

Adelia likes the area around the quad. Even with a garage door company catty-cornered across the street and the organ parts manufacturer and lumberyard two blocks away, the neighborhood is quiet. Renters across the hall and downstairs are friendly enough although contact is limited.

Adelia did not meet her neighbors outside the quad until a few days before. They became acquainted during hours of shoveling required to escape a freak snowfall of more than thirty inches in less than twenty-four hours. Adelia never saw that much white stuff in such a short period, even while spending nine winters in mid-Michigan. In the Shenandoah Valley of Virginia, the effect was paralyzing.

Adelia worked relentlessly the first ten hours to maintain clearance around her car and for her upstairs neighbors who were due back from visiting family on a nearby mountainside farm. One quad family was absent all winter, and the other seemed content to hibernate. Twenty inches of snow later, Adelia turned off the porch light and went to bed.

Next morning, ten more inches reached frighteningly far up her laboriously crafted tunnels. Only the antenna of her neighbors' second car showed now. Although she dug out immediately around her car within an hour, the Toyota seemed hopelessly blocked from the street by extra snow-plowed drifts.

By mid-morning neighbors were working on their own paths, sometimes pausing a moment to exchange slightly breathless observations about the storm.

"Hi, I'm Barbara."

"I'm Adelia. Glad to meet you."

"Sure never seen anything like this."

"Have you lived here long, Barbara?"

"Oh, about seven years. I guess it'll take awhile to get everything moving again. Better get back at it."

"Yeah. Maybe I'll grab a cup of hot chocolate before I start again," Adelia said. "I've got to dig this car out and get to the post office. And I have several meetings across the mountain in the next couple of days."

Receiving cancellation notices that afternoon, Adelia wondered why she thought anyone would hold non-essential meetings in rural areas after a blizzard. That was after walking down three side streets before finding two boys who helped her shovel for four hours to clear the way for her car.

Returning from the post office she cautioned several youngsters digging snow tunnels in the mounds. "You know that snow can collapse really quick," she yelled over the excited chatter and frenzied digging. "Hey," she paused until a red-hatted head turned her way. "Be sure at least one of you is in the clear who can run for help if you need it."

"Yeah, okay," he said, stepping further in to shovel out more snow.

This is life in the area. People caught up in their own projects or activities. Friendly enough, but busy. Adelia is no exception, spending most hours inside the apartment on the telephone and computer setting up meetings with potential clients for her public relations business. She is struggling to live her dream.

Twenty years before, she fell in love with Central Virginia, passing through at the end of a long vacation to the Washington, D.C. area. What she really loved was Monticello, Thomas Jefferson's home in Charlottesville, across the mountain.

However, job-seeking efforts in Virginia resulted only in offers for part-time teaching posts. She accepted a one-year position with James Madison University, well up north in the Shenandoah Valley, but thought the client base for her public relations consulting firm would be closer to Richmond, seventy miles east of Charlottesville on Interstate 64. Waynesboro was a compromise location.

Life in the quad is okay. No complaints except the cost of heating an apartment with absolutely no insulation, leaky windows, and heating vents near the ceiling with no fan to bring warmth down to dwelling level. The downstairs neighbors are absent this winter so no heat comes from below. During the summer, the second floor apartment was almost unbearably hot. Touching anything metal was a distinctive experience. She wore out an ice tea pot.

The public relations business is slow, and Adelia needs something to break the doldrums of routine. Maybe the move to Fairfax Hall can do that.

* * *

Fairfax Hall is east of Route 340, the two-lane, back-road highway that cuts through the far eastern edge of one of six eastern cities named for Revolutionary War hero "Mad" Anthony Wayne. The highway continues north past the former mining area of Crimora and toward her workplace in Harrisonburg. South of Fairfax Hall, Route 340 extends as one of two main entrances into Waynesboro off Interstate 64.

The juncture is three miles west of the interstate's intersection with Afton Mountain, a famous Appalachian Trail dividing point. There, the Skyline Drive from the north gives way to the Blue Ridge Parkway to the south on the trail's scenic 2,168-mile journey from Maine to Georgia. It is not uncommon during the late-spring to early-fall season to see dozens of AT hikers eating at Weasie's Kitchen, picking up mail at the post office, and stocking up on supplies. More than twenty Waynesboro residents volunteer to drive the adventurers in and out of town.

Adelia's new home, a registered national landmark, perches within the boundaries of Basic City, once the independent and larger rival community of Waynesboro. For some time, she thought the large brown building peered over Waynesboro from the western slope of, as locals call it, THE mountain that divides the city and the Shenandoah Valley physically, socially, and psychologically from Central Virginia and its horse country. And, on eastward, from the typically urban Richmond, the James River plantations, historic Williamsburg, and finally the Chesapeake Bay and Atlantic Ocean. After almost eighteen months in the valley—with frequent travels to other parts of Virginia on business and pleasure—Adelia has no doubt that lifestyles of people between the Blue Ridge and Allegheny mountain ranges are different from those outside the valley. Comfortably so.

Actually, Adelia's new view is from a fifteen-hundred-foot bluff, miles from the major slope. Still, at this time in late January, the panorama is wonderful, unhampered by leafless trees. There are few distinctive sights in Waynesboro, but Adelia likes the idea of looking out over the city. The view at night must be spectacular. One major disadvantage to her apartment's location, she muses, is that it faces toward the mountain.

* * *

Driving south now on Route 340, Adelia turned west on the in-town part of Highway 250, the preinterstate route that continues east over Afton Mountain and into Charlottesville. She slowed in congested traffic at the railroad bridge construction. This was unusual on Saturday morning. Rounding a curve, less than a mile later, she discovered the cause. Water.

The three to four inches of rain that inevitably led to slight flooding in local areas also melted the record snow from fourteen days before. The South River—regularly nestled deep within a narrow channel—overspilled its banks, covering the main route and creeping steadily into downtown. Two weeks ago, it seemed like a good idea to pile mountains of snow cleared from the city's streets and parking lots onto the empty land along the river's course. The result today was more than four inches above the nine-and-a-half-foot flood stage.

Adelia saw the watery expanse in time to take the last side street back to Route 340. Driving toward the interstate, she cut back toward town south of the Wayn-Tex and Dupont industrial plants. She could drive into downtown from the south if the water was not over the bridge on Wayne Avenue just before the YMCA.

Sawhorse barriers lined the road, preventing access to side streets leading two to three blocks down to the river. However, Wayne Avenue was clear past the Y, the library, the Episcopalian and Lutheran churches, the majestic homes, the Baptist and Presbyterian churches, the senior citizens housing complex, the city-county building, the parade grounds of Fishburne Military School, a couple of small businesses, and finally the post office. Parking at the post office today was much better than several days earlier when snow removal efforts cleared less than half the parking lanes on both sides, leaving roughly one-and-a-half slushy lanes for traffic.

But this is the valley. People make do under the circumstances, not overly concerned with traffic regulations. They were thankful this day that the heavy rain, no doubt, would deter the meter maid from appointed rounds of enforcing the ten-minute parking limit. Now there was time to review the crazy weather with friends and strangers.

Emptying her post office box, Adelia realized she needed postcard stamps and joined a short line at the counter. Soon she had her purchase and a few minutes to chat with the counterman, Richard.

"I guess the guys are having another rough day delivering the mail," Adelia said. For three days after the largest snowfall since the storm of 1831, postal employees delivered mail only to houses where people provided tunnels from streets to mailboxes. In Staunton, the county seat twelve miles away, hardly anyone moved up and down the numerous hills; only those riding in humvees supplied by the national guard. Some of the humvees got stuck. In Richmond, people who chauffeured essential personnel in four-wheel-drive vehicles sported sweatshirts that read, "I kept the city moving during the blizzard of '96."

"Are y'all running routes today or are you flooded out?" It was good to be in Virginia where her native-Texan use of the southern pronoun drew fewer startled glances than in Michigan.

"Oh, we're getting most of the mail out," Richard replied. "The problem will be getting the trucks back in. I was out a few minutes ago, and the water is already up to the driveway."

Indeed it was. Craving a bag of potato chips to munch while planning the move, Adelia left the post office front entrance and walked around the side, between it and the accountant's office. She walked eastward, toward the river and the grocery just across the next street. While the high crown of the road was dry, the curb edges were inundated with moderately rushing, muddy water, about six inches deep. Fast enough that Adelia elected to try another store.

Starting her nine-year-old Toyota Corolla, which was approaching the quarter-million-mile mark, Adelia turned left at the intersection and drove up the steep roadway which flanks the military school administration building and then the newspaper office. There, last fall, Adelia resuscitated her journalism training and experience of twenty-two years, substituting for staff members on leave for the Thanksgiving holiday. The city's soapbox derby races are held the next street over, she remembered. Waynesboro's derby is second in size only to the event's birthplace, Akron, Ohio.

Topping the hill, she turned right, past the city school administration building and took the side street back onto Highway 250 heading west away from the flood. Lines at the other grocery were longer than usual, no doubt swelled by customers who usually shopped downtown. Setting her two-liter pop bottle and two bags of chips on the conveyor belt, Adelia thought about the best route home to the quad on the other side of the flood. She chatted with another woman picking up a few items.

"You should be able to go out Hopeman Parkway to Route 340 without hitting any high water," the woman said. "We didn't have any trouble there during the 1969 flood." That natural disaster was the prime topic of comparison this day. Hurricane Camille came northeast from the Gulf of Mexico, triggering a series of thunderstorms over the Blue Ridge Mountains. Water rose to over eight feet in Waynesboro's downtown area as the South River spilled almost six feet over flood stage.

Receiving a "good luck" from the cashier, Adelia walked to her still-dripping car and headed north on the suggested road. It was about time, she thought, to rescue Mollie. Her cocker spaniel would appreciate the reprieve from a longer-than-expected stay in her doghouse, nestled in the yard which was a growing sea of mud as the thirty inches of snow gradually disappeared.

* * *

Eight hours and sixteen inches into the blizzard, the white cocker with brown spots followed Adelia down the second floor steps onto the front porch. Adelia retrieved the shovel to continue clearing the small stoop and keeping a small path open to the car and a little beyond. One thing she learned right away in Michigan—having grown up in the sparse, shallow snows of Texas—you cannot let the snow get ahead of you.

Jumping suddenly to avoid being scooped up with the snow, Mollie landed head-first down in the snow drift that was even with the porch. Only her brown-patched tail was showing, and it was not wagging. Before Adelia could rescue her, the cocker jumped out on the path, bounded up the steps, and ran in the door leading to the inside stair passage. It was several hours before she ventured out again. However, she soon learned to crawl out gingerly onto the snow closest to the building, especially to retrieve bread crumbs Adelia threw out for the birds.

* * *

Adelia was unsure of the suggested route around the flood, having traveled that way only once before. Traffic backed up behind another water-covered road was not a pleasant sight. However, Adelia is a seasoned traveler with a surprising instinct for direction. She took the next side street into completely unknown territory, hoping drivers of the few cars moving that way knew where they were going—and were headed the same direction as she. Largely uneducated reckoning convinced her that, at worst, she would surface on the high street just west of the flooded area and have to retrace her route through downtown, onto Route 340, and cross the railroad track on the Second Street bridge. The closer Fourth Street bridge was blocked by its own reconstruction, and the Seventh Street crossing might be blocked by normal local flooding.

Fortunately, Adelia's new route went directly to the Second Street extension. Unfortunately, the lowest point was under water. Minutes passed while cars and trucks in her own lane, and in the on-coming one, negotiated the low ford. There was time enough to review the dangers of driving through flowing water, backed by memories of her father's white-knuckled undertaking on a flooded highway in West Texas. Pre-teen Adelia and other car occupants saw nothing but water for over half a mile.

Adelia watched carefully and decided she could make it, though the Toyota had a low clearance. At worst, she would wind up against a softball backstop in North Park. The water here was not raging or deep. Saying a short prayer, she plunged cautiously ahead —and made it.

Arriving home minutes later, she retrieved a much-less-than-white Mollie and chatted with a neighbor a few minutes about the flood. Ending her day's adventure, she made a sandwich to complement the chips and poured the soda over a cup of crackling ice to complete the lunch necessities. She started room diagrams for her new apartment while catching up quickly on the plot of the A&E movie.

Chapter 2

Living in three rooms on the middle floor of Fairfax Hall was not routine. Adelia and Mollie were alone on the second floor, two-hundred-sixty feet across, north to south, with a seventy-foot wing perpendicular to the main hall on the north side.

She had not asked her landlord. However, Adelia thought the unusual living arrangements lowered insurance rates on the property while two partners held several buildings on the seventeen acres as an investment. It also brought in income. A couple with two young children had a suite on the first floor, and two twenty-something guys lived above Adelia on the third.

Walking up the main stairway a week after the flood, Adelia paused on the landing to peer into a small room where mattresses, carpet scraps, and drapes were flung haphazardly about. Just ahead was the entrance of the building's central perpendicular wing where the maintenance man, John Hiller, and his wife, Tilley, lived. Guarding the door sleepily was Baby, an old, overweight dog of indeterminate breeds. A few feet away, an industrial-kitchen-sized pan of kitty litter lay in front of the railing, affording its currently absent feline a view down into the back of the lobby. Two balusters were missing. If allowed to roam freely, Mollie's curiosity could lead to a twelve-foot fall. More likely, the cocker, who spent her first year in a house full of cats, would go find this one, hoping for a playmate. A few stairs and several strides more, past a closed and locked door, Adelia walked through open doors into the second floor hallway.

The floor was covered in serviceable, but deteriorating linoleum. The walls shed bits of wallpaper and plaster. The hallway appeared to stretch half a football field's length to the left along the main axis of the building. Adelia's rooms were to the right, four steps down and just past a small angular room where damaged walls showed their underlying plaster-on-lath structure. The mottled ceiling suggested substantial water damage. However, the still-polished wood floor showed little regular or irregular wear, its peril revealed only by another large kitchen pan—at the moment, dry.

Adelia tended to notice details like these. "Was it her late high school and early college training as a journalist?" she thought. Or was she wondering how to tell her mother—who clings to the security of traditional neighborhoods of modest, middle class houses—about her new, definitely nontraditional dwelling?

"Furthermore, she wondered, "why was this stretch of the second floor lower? The difference was not noticeable when viewing the three-story expanse from outside.

The apartment needed additional cleaning after an apparent general pick-up by John in preparation for her coming. The large piece of dark green, well-used carpet covering most of the floor in Room 216-A would do for a while. The nondescript linoleum in the bathroom was in one piece, and the carpet in Room 216-B was newer, with padding, and wall-to-wall. Walls and ceilings in each room displayed some surface cracks but were in better shape than other rooms Adelia had seen. The front half of 216-A was empty. However, the obviously new cabinet-sink combination on the bathroom side near the back provided counter space, a wash-up area, and some storage for the kitchen.

"Where did John get this beautiful mahogany table with intricately carved front and thick Queen Anne curve legs?" thought Adelia. "What a rich contrast with the spartan quarters!"

Bringing in a small, early-vintage refrigerator on a hand trolley, John said, nodding at the table, "I thought it'd be big enough for the microwave oven and hot plate."

"And my crock pot and can opener," Adelia responded, with a tone reflecting more love of adventure than dismay over a makeshift kitchen.

Peeking in the refrigerator's freezer compartment, Adelia remained resolute, although this upper portion would hold hardly more than a half gallon of ice cream, three ice trays, and two small packages of meat. As he connected the appliance, John said, "Oh yeah! Don't try to plug too many things into these outlets."

Adelia and John's quick survey of several rooms down the hall yielded sets of drapes that adequately shielded the one big window in each large room. The faded yellow-and-other-earth-tones print fabric was merely utilitarian, but there were only small holes in the linings. The petite bathroom window was too high to require a covering. More interesting to Adelia during the scavenger hunt were glimpses of randomly desolate rooms. "I can hardly wait to poke around some more," Adelia thought as John left. Cleaning her own apartment was in order first.

In the kitchen/living room closet, Adelia found a scrap of yellow carpet that fit the small hallway between the two main rooms. The compartment's space from front to back was so shallow that only a few garments, their hangers twisted sideways, would fit.

The bedroom/office closet was much larger, with a good supply of hooks and the expected clothes rod. Electrical outlets in the large room were modern, offering hope of handling her computer and printer along with a desk lamp, bedside table lamp, alarm clock/radio combination and a small stereo. "Why did the wall on the far right—the best place for the queen size bed—bulge out five-and-a-half inches?" she wondered.

Two hours later the apartment was clean enough. It was late January and time to move in. Several members of Adelia's Sunday school class agreed to help.

* * *

At first, the previous night's snowstorm seemed the biggest challenge. Adelia sighed in gratitude at the dedication of volunteers as a pickup, van, and several cars crawled up the slight slope of the driveway off Reservoir Street. Thankfully, the snow was hardly a dusting, about an eighth inch.

Adelia's possessions consisted of a cedar chest inherited from her mother, a light butcher block table crafted by her father, a bed frame and queen mattress set, a small computer desk, five drawers of filing cabinets, several small or collapsible tables and bookcases, some lamps, a microwave oven, a small television, and various boxes of clothes, knickknacks, and kitchenware. And a thousand pounds of books and photo albums.

"Why not take advantage of the building's large dumbwaiter?" she thought. Back David's truck up to the north porch, basement level, and it was only a short hallway to the tall, eighteen-inch deep by four-foot wide conveyance. Unfortunately, the contraption was raised and lowered manually by rope pulleys.

Lance stepped gamely into the compartment with the first pile of boxes, pulling the ropes downward, hand over hand. Auxiliary rope tugging by his team was largely ineffectual; Lance reached the second floor nearing exhaustion. Adelia was sorting through boxes in the apartment down the hall, unaware of the heroic efforts.

Experimentation with lighter loads revealed how to work the dumbwaiter without a human rider. "It looks to me that all we have to do is bring the ropes out and pull from here," Frank said, demonstrating. Linda and Geri quickly helped. An hour later, as everyone else rested on mattresses found in nearby rooms, Bob called to Adelia, "Let's go get the rest of your things." Coming through the front entrance and up the main stairway they discovered a longer portage, but lighter labor.

Weary with accomplishment, the crew quickly declined pizza and pop, preferring to hurry on to a busy Saturday schedule of more appealing family activities.

"If we have another snow, you'll have to bring the kids for sledding," Adelia offered as if to compensate for thanks registered only in word. "There's a great hill on the side of the building."

Waving goodbye, Adelia walked through the small parking lot and down the gradual slope to pet two horses grazing several yards inside the pasture fence. Somewhat embarrassed, she tried to neigh softly enough not to attract attention. Her dad was so good at this, entertaining the family as they passed horse farms in Kentucky on the 1950s driving vacations before interstate highways. "Why couldn't she project a more horsy sound?" she thought.

Still, the horses were encouraged—or hungry—and moved her way slowly. Adelia carefully avoided the probably electrified taut wire just inside the top rail, leaning over to rub their noses and pet their cheeks. She always loved horses. Her experience, though, was limited to one or two rides a year. These were from stables where, after plodding—necks adroop—for thirty or forty minutes along a well-defined trail in single file, the horses saw the barn and broke into a canter. Promising to bring carrots next time, Adelia left to gather her keys and head to Tastee-Freeze for a quick lunch before returning to the quad for Mollie.

* * *

Unloading boxes and arranging furniture was fun. Adelia enjoyed the packing and unpacking chores, occasionally amazing her friends by helping them pack for their moves. It was a challenge to find just the right sized and shaped objects to fit into every cranny of each box. After one move, her favorite salt and pepper shakers were missing for months until she searched a back closet to get crystal out for company. The shakers were safely fitted into extra compartments of the original packing box.

In seven moves, Adelia lost only one item, even when packing three complete sets of dishes and a fifty-two-piece collection of mugs. At its peak, the collection included a mug from every vacation location, including one of thimble size from Hampton Court near London, England.

Today, Mollie spent the unpacking time sometimes shadowing her box-carrying mistress and often shying away from randomly placed, tottering stacks of books—and from bundles of clothes swinging from suitcases to the clothes bar in the closet. Sometimes she merely sat in a corner of inactivity with a cute—was it confounded?—and trusting look. As long as her "mom" was there with frequent encouraging words, Mollie was okay.

The hardest chore was assembling the bed frame and maneuvering the queen size mattresses into place in the confined space. However, Adelia was accustomed to working alone. She proudly remembered her success last year in putting together that computer desk all by herself, though the instructions said two people were needed.

The most engaging task was arranging the bedroom/office so that the two areas were separated by a pleasing barrier, while thirty or so unpacked boxes were stashed more or less out of sight. The challenge was a pleasure for Adelia. Once she fell in love with a small, over-the-garage apartment with sloping eaves where two pieces of furniture were too tall to fit against the walls. So the bookcase sat out from the wall in the bedroom, providing a partial separation for a small office. Space behind the free-standing china cabinet held boxes of seldom-used items in the second bedroom-turned dining room. "Where did she get this organizational ability?" she wondered. Perhaps it was from years of working jigsaw puzzles.

This time she stacked boxes of unneeded items out from one corner, placed the computer desk and a large bookcase in front of the largest open side, and started her bedroom-from-office barrier on the other. Adelia set a bookcase near the head of the bed to double as a bedside table and, next to it, lined up the cedar chest, covered with her souvenir blanket throw from New Zealand. She finished the barrier with another short bookcase and a cardboard, two-drawer chest of purple floral. Another tall bookcase and filing cabinets fit nicely along the walls of the office. There was just enough room in the bedroom for a small chest of drawers, yet to be purchased, and the clothes hamper fit neatly against the wall between the interior door and closet. It was all quite different, she imagined, from the dorm mother's carefully made bed, doily covered dresser, and dressing table with perfume atomizer and facial powder jars.

Turning to the living room-kitchen space, Adelia remembered her idea to use a single bed from one of the rooms down the hall as a couch substitute. She mentally gauged its length while arranging her own furniture. A two-shelf wooden microwave stand would serve as an end table. Her rocking chair, floor lamp and nicest bookcase completed the living area. She imagined the dorm mother's curved-back sofa and overstuffed chair—with doilies, a floor model television, and several etagerés with porcelain figurines and boxes, and a book or two.

Adelia's small television and VCR sat on another microwave stand, positioned between the refrigerator and large table and also holding assorted pots and pans. Behind this, shelves of a tall bookcase provided a pantry. Elated, Adelia discovered that her treasured bedside table fit between the interior door and closet. She bought the fourteen-inch-square, two-tiered, slightly worn cherry table in an antique store in Muskogee, Oklahoma. Thus ended a nine-month search to find just the right item for the small space beside the new cherry, four-poster bed in her Remus, Michigan house.

Most of the fine furniture was gone now. Selling it was easier and cheaper than storing it or moving it eight hundred miles from Michigan to unknown lodgings in Virginia on a limited budget. She sold most of it to the financial director and secretary of a camp she sometimes attended in Northern Michigan. Now whenever Adelia visited the Jamisons overnight, she felt at home sleeping in her former bedstead.

Adelia retained only the cedar chest, butcher block, five bookcases, and a few must-keep personal items. Still, the jammed U-Haul trailer was a questionable load for her aging Toyota, especially through the Allegheny mountains. Characteristically, Adelia carefully studied the possible routes and chose the Pennsylvania Turnpike. It had no long steep grades like the West Virginia Turnpike which Adelia had traveled on her many trips to Virginia from Oklahoma and Kentucky since 1976.

During that bicentennial-year vacation, she fell in love with Washington, D.C. and Colonial Williamsburg, in addition to Monticello and the renaissance-man nature of Thomas Jefferson. She enthusiastically shared those sights on a four-day whirlwind trip around Virginia with her Michigan friend, Jennifer, who shared the U-Haul adventure and unpacking chores at her first Virginia home, the quad.

The many books, pictures, and memorabilia of Adelia's Jefferson collection would stay packed during her time at Fairfax Hall. All were ensconced in the bedroom pile of boxes except the year-round wreath of Virginia ornaments she substituted for a traditional six-foot Christmas tree the holiday before.

"Enough reminiscing," she thought. Time to explore the second floor while finding the couch.

Twenty nine dorm-like rooms lined the main hallway. "Average, about twelve by fifteen feet," Adelia reckoned. There was also a ganged toilet and shower room featuring fixtures in various phases of disrepair. Each room was a different size and configuration. Some were simple rectangles with shallow closets and large, single windows. Some had wall projections and sloping ceilings. Each held an assortment of partially hung drapes, ill-fitting carpet, mattresses, often upturned bed frames, and small—always green—metal end tables. Wallpaper, plaster, and pieces of ceiling bulged, gaped, peeled and dangled. Water damage was often evident.

A room in the northwest corner was especially shabby. Dark stains marred the ceiling, and the cornice sagged in one corner, while the baseboard crumbled near the closet. The well-worn wall revealed various stages of decoration—layers of paint and wallpaper and a gold stucco-like surface over plaster along the lathwork. Adelia shuddered as she walked back through the doorway into the hall.

On the other end, some rooms' floors sloped noticeably. They reminded Adelia of a former colleague's cartoon in which the golf-putting character said, "I have to get a new office. This one slants to the right."

In the middle of the second floor expanse, on the west front, was a succession of tiny rooms, including a cabinet-lined area, that ended on the flat porte-cochere roof with its sadly deteriorating balustrade. Adelia walked outside, avoiding the puddles and mindful of the spongy flooring, to find a satellite dish and an elevated view of the front parking area and pasture beyond. "Probably a good place for sunbathing," Adelia mused.

Turret-like structures on either end of the main axis featured rounded rooms, devoid of furnishings but not without scars of maintenance neglect. On the hall's north end a wing doglegged to the right; Adelia decided to call it the north perpendicular. A walk down its length revealed more rooms in various stages of shambles. A large armoire half-covered the window in one, its angle betraying hasty positioning. A twist of the wrist on an old doorknob failed to open a closet jammed tantalizingly into the wall just as the hall took a slight jog to the left a few feet before a ganged bathroom.

Although she saw many possibilities for her couch, Adelia continued to the third floor, intrigued by the potential finds. Ascending the stairs next to the dumb waiter, she emerged on the

Elizabeth Tidwell

next floor which, at first, looked like hers. However, the rooms varied more in size and sometimes were located on narrow passages off the main hall. Furnishings were more sparse and states of disrepair less evident. Walls of the room across from the south turret were unfinished, revealing the brick back of the fireplace next door and the wooden studs of the exterior walls, unblemished by disintegrating plaster. In the turret room, Adelia tried without success to read the few bits of poem not erased by unknown years of bad weather:

```
        De   o   F     ax
        liv s   n  m m
        Lan    rne    ket
        def     sc  ry
```

At the hall's opposite end, Adelia traversed a short, low tunnel, sharply angled from the main passage, into the north turret. Here the window-like openings were screened. "This will make a nice warm-weather party area for the guys and their guests," Adelia thought. The north perpendicular held no surprises.

Backtracking toward the central stairs, Adelia discovered a small enclosed, upward stairway she assumed led to the attic. Climbing eighteen steps, her gaze rose to the soaring rafters above then fell to the flooring on either side of a central platform. Below, scraps of plastic and paper trash draped ceiling braces of the rooms below. Littering the platform was a selection of wood pieces, hardware, plastic containers and more light-green, metal tables.

Stepping over what looked to be an electrical wire about shin height, Adelia gazed up the next set of boxed steps. She pushed a horizontal door further aside at the top and stepped into a riot of wood and paint chips on the bottom level of the cupola. The closely spaced picket fence-like walls broke at waist height into eight sides of thirty-inch high openings joined by corner posts on the way to another ceiling.

Ladder-like steps led to another, partially open hatch. Lifting the cover to the left, Adelia stepped up. Still only shoulders above the lip of the opening, she had a close-up view of the even more chaotic condition of second level flooring. The walls were slightly higher and more solid here, topped also by taller openings, broken only by four-inch round columns badly in need of scraping and paint. Directly overhead was the shallow conical roof of the cupola.

Seconds later, Adelia learned quickly to avoid several boardless floor spots while enjoying a three-hundred-sixty-degree view of the Fairfax Hall setting.

The city of Waynesboro spread far out to the west, nearly flat to the horizon. To the north, the low forest was backed by a distant mauve mountain rising gradually from the western edge to blend with the Blue Ridge height. A slope of close-packed, mostly leafless trees looked like tall brush, partially obscuring the high eastern mountains. To the south, tops of taller trees pointed to a bluer mountain, sloping much like the one to the north, but not so far away.

Closer in, Adelia saw the familiar sights, now with a bird's eye view: The pasture in front. The north perpendicular, beyond and to the right of the turret. Other Fairfax structures in the back, including a modern orange-brick, two-story classroom building and a half-timbered, stucco-faced gym to the left. Houses aligned across Reservoir Street beyond the south turret.

Most immediate was the roof of large, rusting metal shingles. Red-brick chimneys perched along the slopes of the high hips. There were more chimneys than obvious fireplaces inside. Most were capped.

The dilapidated state of the cupola floor did not invite more prolonged sightseeing. Carefully, Adelia descended the steps through each hatch. The upper step of the lower flight sounded more hollow than the others.

Reaching the attic floor, Adelia picked up a metal table and decided she had explored enough for awhile. She grabbed a single bed frame and set of mattresses from the room across the hall from her apartment.

* * *

Entering the front door several evenings later, after a shift on her new part-time job, Adelia chanced upon the handyman. "Living in this huge building must have been pretty spooky before the rest of us got here," Adelia said.

Suddenly the two children of the first floor came across the lobby, Joy hesitantly on skates and Bo confidently riding a tricycle.

"You know, this reminds me of a movie," Adelia laughed.

"*The Shining*," John said immediately, as both remembered the caretaker's small child pedaling his tricycle down the halls of the remote, snowbound resort hotel in Stephen King's horror film.

John pointed out the clock just inside the main entrance—to the right, over the door to a small parlor. Time stopped at nine-fifty. To the right of the door, a mirror at hair-checking height hid a cabinet for keys. The plaque nearby read, "Fairfax Hall. National Register of Historic Places. September 9, 1982." The carpeted parlor was empty now with only a small fireplace opening in the corner.

Stepping farther from the entrance, Adelia took a closer look at the sparsely furnished lobby. "It must have been very different for the students," Adelia surmised. Now there was a black faux-leather couch in front of the fireplace and a matching chair to the right. A triptych mirror over the mantel reflected little but wooden columns carefully spaced throughout the large open room.

Up three stairs behind the sitting area, empty glass-enclosed bookcases framed a vacant platform, expanding on either side of a closed door. Adelia opened it and descended three steps to find a small room with a few plain wall shelves. Across the room was another door, this one open. Adelia went down four more steps into a larger room lined with wall-to-wall, finely crafted bookshelves sporting a variety of knickknacks, trophies, and neon bar signs. In the middle of the room was a pool table.

Exiting a door to the right into a hall, Adelia spied the building's rear entrance to the left, past several doors—some open, some closed. She was too tired to explore the spaces behind them, even dismissing the intriguing floor-level, three-foot-square door just past the pool room to the right. She followed black and white linoleum tiles through a zigzag back to the front of the building and found herself at the foot of the main stairs.

Retrieving Mollie, she used the need for a brief dog walk to explore the area out the back entrance. As she ducked under the stairway leading to the handyman's back door, Adelia thought, "This would make a grand entrance to the most posh modern deck. Why attach such a nice stair to the deteriorating middle wing?"

Pulling the remains of a discarded sandwich from Mollie's close-clamped jaws, she led the cocker to a grassy area between the two perpendicular wings to do her business. She discovered a long, less than half-story structure almost against the main building.

* * *

The next afternoon, obsessed by need for her famous seafood pizza, Adelia checked out the oven in an industrial-size kitchen across from the pool room. The oven wall also backed a multi-tiered warming unit. Nearby, a small alcove sheltered large mixers flanking spacious plastic bins, two of which still contained flour and sugar. Next to these a large institutional-size refrigerator freezer contained a few sandwich fixings and a lot of beer.

Stainless steel shelving and large sinks offered room for banquet-size dish washing on another side. Counter and cabinet space languished along the other wall below once well-stocked shelves, she assumed. They were littered now with a mishmash of pans, utensils and boxes. The island in the room's middle nestled beneath overhead racks for pots and pans.

The oven looked simple enough, but Adelia found the room overwhelming so she assembled her pizza upstairs. Mollie was eager to help, serving as clean up crew for any morsels that dropped on the floor during the preparation.

While the pizza baked, Adelia explored storage rooms, including a walk-in freezer, absolutely empty, even of holding racks. The spaces were apparently unused for some time and would take considerable cleanup. Uneven flooring, scattered debris and shelves of assorted rust-edged cans—their contents unrevealed by badly stained labels—encouraged Adelia to exit the area through a door just short of the back entrance. She opened a door across the hall to find a room cluttered with assortments of newer picnic and sporting equipment and a small refrigerator freezer.

Time to check the pizza. "Just in time," Adelia sighed in relief as she opened the oven to a wave of heat.

She had barely negotiated the doorknob—after carefully climbing the stairs while juggling the pizza-covered cookie sheet, spatula, and oven mitt—when Bo and Joy appeared. Their curious and imploring eyes were too hard to resist, Adelia decided, and she handed over small slivers of her handiwork on plain white napkins. Off her young neighbors went, with enthusiastic "Thanks."

Pizza, a TV basketball game, and a short nap later, Adelia decided her initial success with the oven could be followed by a cookie bake. It was time to contribute to the snack room at work. Although her favorite recipe allowed for creativity with color and shape, she decided to keep it simple—uncolored dough flattened into irregular shapes with the heel of her hand. Fortunately, the oven held two cookie sheets side-by-side. Adelia took her bowl of dough and necessary extra utensils and trays with her to make three double batches.

She slid the first two sheets in and went out through the other kitchen door to find a room full of stainless steel buffet and serving equipment. Exiting the opposite door, she entered the dining/ballroom, a beautiful mahogany panorama of wood-paneled columns —almost against the walls—regularly spaced between a hardwood floor and ceiling. Long, narrow floor planks stretched north to south from interior door to a twin of the lobby fireplace. Thin wood strips formed the wainscoting of the high walls. Beaded boards filled the space between exposed ceiling beams and purlins running east to west.

"Oops!" Adelia exclaimed aloud. Time to check the cookies.

A few minutes of work, and Adelia was ready to explore the several doorways of the dining room. They led to glassed-in porches on the front and south end of the building which would be worth exploring in more detail later.

By the time the second batch of cookies was done, Joy and Bo appeared in the kitchen.

"Watcha making?" asked Bo. "Can we have some?"

"Shhh! Don't be so pushy," said Joy. "Maybe we can help."

"As a matter of fact," Adelia said, "you can help me get these cookies off so I can make more. Say, if we can find something to put them on, maybe we can give you some cookies to take back for supper, for your parents, too."

Bo looked pleased as Joy looked around for something to use.

"Here's a good size pan," Adelia said skeptically, wondering how long it sat around unused. "Oh, and there's some foil we can use to line it."

As Joy cleared cookies off the second sheet, Adelia let Bo put some remaining dough on the first. She smiled as he struggled with the unfamiliar task of shaping it. Joy, starting on her cleared one, was more adept at traditional baking techniques and tried some different designs.

Sliding the two trays into the oven and grabbing the cookie pan, Adelia said, "Let's go down and surprise your folks."

Daley opened the door to the family's suite. It was to the left of the lobby on Adelia's end of the building but the opposite side of the hall. Adelia managed only a glance at the kitchen and living room as the children proudly presented dessert, and she quickly begged off to check on the last batch.

Mollie was thrilled with the late afternoon baking since these were her favorite cookies. It was the only food Adelia ever saw her make a special effort—climbing off the floor onto a chair—to snatch one. As she finished slipping cookies into a gallon ziplock bag for work, she retrieved a smaller bag to contain a few of Bo's and Joy's creations.

Putting Mollie on her leash, Adelia went downstairs to leave the cookies at the family's distinctive double door and to spend a few minutes exploring the first floor north hall. To the right, at the end was a glass door obscured by lacy curtains and a room-dividing screen placed close to the opening. When unlocked the door opened into the library of the Montessori school that used the first floor of the north perpendicular. The next door opened onto the wing, just before the back stairs to the second floor. The doors along the wing were locked.

Along the main hall were two plain rooms, probably former offices. One contained a simple wood table, a faded-yellow stuffed chair, and a big television-size packing box. A quick glance at its contents revealed a disarray of school class pictures and negatives. Adelia must give those closer scrutiny later. There was a ganged restroom behind the next door, much nicer than the ones upstairs.

Just before the lobby on the opposite side was the old reception/office area.

Mollie whined a warning so Adelia led her out the front door, across the wide porch, and down the steps into the grassy area backed by rhododendron which grew along the porch off the dining hall. Walking down the slope next to the flagpole terrace, Adelia noticed a ragged NASCAR flag at the top of the mast. She unleashed Mollie near the pasture fence and looked for the big roan horse, but it apparently sheltered in the shed for the night. Mollie was tracing a darting squirrel trail toward the north end of the building so Adelia hurried after to leash her and enter the door on the lower level of the two-story porch. She made a mental note to explore this basement area soon.

* * *

Heading toward the dumbwaiter on the lowest floor two days later, Adelia's attention was drawn to the gaping irregular hole in the wall just ahead. Beyond the stone edge was a slight slope of dark red-brown earth, punctuated with bits of bricks and rock. The dirt reached to the level of the floor above, Adelia observed and thought aloud, "So apparently there is no basement all the way across."

Next to the hole, she entered a room darkened by nursery-type curtains over small windows along the back wall at ground level. Adelia rubbed her banged knee in disgust and shook her head in wonderment as her eyes adjusted to the faint light. Modern vanity tops and bathtubs were scattered haphazardly across the floor.

On the northwest side of the building were two former classrooms, evidenced by their mottled blackboards, erased more by water damage than a teacher's final attention to detail. An exterior door with sidelights concluded the main hallway at the point where Montessori space began the perpendicular wing above.

Around the corner into the basement perpendicular, the right-hand wall was covered by large, framed panes of ornate spider glass. Noticing the hinges on either side, Adelia found the middle opening and unveiled the metal doors and combination locks of old-fashioned post office boxes. Inside the room were counters and shelves, empty now but large enough to hold many packages. There was nothing in the post office boxes but desiccated bug carcasses.

The room next door held deep galvanized sinks and washer and dryer connections. Other rooms on the hall may have been narrow classrooms or study areas. They were empty now.

* * *

Resuming exploration of the first floor office wing a few days later, Adelia first admired the arched window over the front office counter. However, the apparently elaborate brass grille surrounding it was cheap facing available in any lumber/hardware store. Blueprints splaying from a banker's box at the back of the office were much more interesting. They showed that the area she investigated before was the main basement. Otherwise there was only a small area beneath the porch on the south side.

As she looked at plans of the upper floors, Adelia had another observation. "It looks like the building underwent a major upgrade in plumbing, electricity and a sprinkler system before the state moved in," Adelia mused aloud.

"Yeah, you really have to watch that sprinkler system. Occasionally it goes off in one room or another," said John, coming up behind her and looking over her shoulder at the blueprints.

Adelia jumped a little and flipped back to the basement diagram. "What's this little room here?" she asked.

Holding up his hammer, John said, "Follow me."

He led Adelia across the lobby, through the ballroom, and onto the enclosed porch where he picked up a trap door fitted neatly into the flooring. Adelia descended the steps carefully, noticing the stone-lined room more out the corners of her eyes until she reached the bottom.

"Welcome to the carpenter's shop," said John.

She inhaled the still pungent odor of wood shavings and lightly stroked the planks waiting on a modern table saw. She spotted age-clouded jars of nails and screws sitting along the wall shelves as she heard John open the door through the stone foundation to the outside.

It was almost one o'clock. She could almost taste the fresh-baked turkey and Swiss cheese sandwich she planned for lunch. Mollie would approve.

The old man drove a late-model black Buick up the semicircular drive just after sunset on the warm March evening. He parked right in front of the old porte-cochere, ignoring traditional parking places across the drive. He half swung, half pulled his legs from under the steering wheel and out the driver's door.

"What's this building?" he asked Adelia. "How many people in there? How long has this been here? Can I go in and look around?" He panted with the effort but conveyed no reason for his interest.

Adelia drew the leashed Mollie closer to her and assumed a posture of interested caution. "I don't know that much about its history. I've only lived here a few weeks," she replied. "It was built in the 1890s as a resort hotel and was a girls prep school for over fifty years."

She paused, calculating how much information to give the stranger. "Several families live here now while two owners look for a buyer for the complex." She continued with authority, "There are some children settling down for the night. It'd be better for you to come back during the day."

He nodded. "I was just interested. I heard there was a valuable locket lost here—and never found. I wondered what happened, what was done—you know—to check the place out." He turned to get back in his car.

"Been staying on The Lawn over at the university. Need to get back home to Buckingham. Maybe I'll see you again sometime when I come by."

"Strange man, interesting tidbit," thought Adelia, an avid mystery fan. The next Saturday, she went to the library for more information.

Chapter 3

He stumbled along, never seeming to make any progress. The muddy ooze sucked at his boots with every step. He tripped on the ragged lower edge of a boulder. It had never been there before. A brick dislodged as his shoulder hit the side, then another and another and. . . .

"Grandpa. Grandpa. Grandpa, Sir," Jud said, with increasing anxiety.

"Wha. What." Sandy Abern awoke with a start to see a worried military cadet sitting across from him at a corner table of the hotel lobby. "Must have fallen asleep," he said, trying to shake it off. "Didn't mean to scare you. What time is it? Is Margaret here yet?"

"No, Grandpa. Her train won't arrive for another hour. If it's on time, for once."

"If it doesn't get caught in the tunnel. The big boulder!"

"That was a dream, Grandpa." He reached toward his arm, but drew back. "You're okay. Aunt Margaret's okay. Here, have another drink of your sarsparilla," he said, nudging the glass closer to his grandfather's slightly shaking right hand.

Sandy wrinkled his nose. He really wanted something stronger, especially after another episode of the familiar nightmare. But it would not do to drink in front of the boy—or to greet Margaret with rummy breath.

"You look so nice in your uniform, Jud."

"Yes, sir. I won't have time to change for parade dress after the train gets in," he explained. "And I guess Aunt Margaret will be pretty impressed, too."

"I wish your dad could of gone to Fishburne. You're getting one fine education at that military school," he said, looking appreciatively at the tall, ramrod straight teen.

"Daddy had already been to war. Not officially, though, as a soldier," Jud reminded him. "He went up to Phillipi with the ambulance corps to help carry supplies. Got caught in the action and lost his leg. That's what he told me, but he never gave me any details."

A flash of teen angst broke through, but Jud hurried on as he saw the first crease of resentment frame Sandy's mouth.

"Grandma said he came back and spent days in his room—wouldn't let anyone go in. Ordered her to bring him supplies," he said, his voice building with excitement. "He finally came out with an artificial leg, he called it. Made a lot of them for the soldiers. Got a patent in 1871 and started up a big business in Richmond after the war." His memory ended with considerable pride.

"He was only eighteen years old when his leg was amputated, one of the first of many," Sandy reflected morosely. "The war was hard. I don't know how we survived here in Waynesboro after Sheridan." Jud nodded, remembering his history lessons, as Sandy continued.

"He caught us just west in Fishersville. Had forty-five thousand men. We never had a chance. Then they destroyed all the crops and storage, slaughtered all the animals."

They fell silent. Jud looked around at the Bruce Hotel's famous mahogany stair railing, rising all the way to the third floor. At the stone top of the card table with its mosaic pattern of a chess board. At the sheet music of tunes by Stephen Foster on the piano.

"Used to have big paintings up there on the wall," Sandy said, awakening again to see Jud's wandering gaze. "One oil painting showed the first people here—Indians, the Shawnee, digging up provisions at a big larder. They called this area 'Daughter of the Stars'," he said, remembering the folk lore.

"Had a copy of the 1736 land grant from King George the Second to William Beverly, too. He sold just a little piece of it to Joseph

Tees. This area, from down by the river to Gospel Hill, was known as Teesville until 1825." Jud listened politely.

"Come to think of it, this was the site of the Widow Tees's Tavern," Sandy continued. "The old story is that George Washington once stopped here. Said the food was the sorriest he ever encountered but the bed was good," he chuckled.

"Mr. Roller said Teesville became Waynesborough when so many Pennsylvanians who fought with Anthony Wayne in the Revolutionary War came in," Jud said, contributing part of a Fishburne lesson.

"Mad Anthony Wayne," Sandy affirmed. "Rode up and down from Pennsylvania to Tennessee. Even went to Georgia and Mississippi fighting Indians. I hear there are five or six towns named for him up and down the valleys. And a few out west, too."

"Did you ever meet anyone famous, Grandpa?" Jud leaned forward in anticipation.

"Well, I missed Andrew Jackson and John C. Calhoun," Sandy said. "I was only about four-years-old. But I did see James Fillmore once at Wayne Tavern. Got back in town with my old mule, Sassy, just in time. Been delivering a load up on the Blue Ridge."

"James who?" Jud was baffled.

"You know. He was president in the early fifties."

"That was a little before my time," Jud admonished.

"That's true. You were born in sixty-six. Helped Waynesboro hit the big five-oh-oh mark in population," Sandy said brightly. "The year after we lost the war," he sighed.

"Tell me about your work in the tunnel," Jud said quickly to change the subject.

"Not much to it," Sandy said. "Albert and me had to walk through the tunnel before every train, checking for fallen rocks, debris and animals. Those deer loved to go in there and eat the moss off the rails. There was times I thought we'd never shoo them out in time.

"We didn't have to worry much about rocks," he said, despite his recurring nightmare. "About a third of the tunnel was lined with bricks, one-hundred-fifty-thousand of them, supposed to be." Jud gave an appreciative low whistle.

"The rest was natural rock. Some of the hardest real estate in the world, one engineer said. It's granite, you know, and greenstone and quartz," Sandy continued, reassuring himself further. "Sometimes, though, large rocks, even boulders, fell."

Since he seemed to enjoy the reverie, Jud let him continue uninterrupted.

"It was the water I hated most," Sandy said, "especially in the winter. If a train surprised us, Albert and me had to lie down in that icy water between the rails. There wasn't any room on the sides," he said with resigned resentment.

"The construction engineer thought the elliptical shape would be stronger and more eco . . .nomical," he stuttered a bit over the word. "But it was only twelve to seventeen feet wide. Just enough most of the way for the engine to pass through."

"Yes, Sir. Mr. Tollman spent two days in class telling us about how it was constructed," Jud said. "That Frenchman who used to work for Napoleon. . . ."

"Crozet," Sandy picked it up. "Hired by the government in Richmond to build four tunnels through the Blue Ridge. They knew, even in the forties, they'd have to move troops and supplies into the valley during a war."

"This tunnel was the longest, right?" asked Jud, urging him on.

"By a long shot. The others were less than a thousand feet; the one at Greenwood is only five-hundred thirty-six," Sandy said, disdainfully. "The Afton, Blue Ridge, Rockfish Gap—whatever you want to call this one—it's almost forty-three-hundred feet, four-fifths mile. Longest in the world."

"Crozet was a genius," offered Jud.

"And very patient," Sandy added. "There were so many problems."

"Yes, sir," Jud affirmed. "Mr. Tollman said they had trouble cutting enough lumber to bridge the six deep ravines from the Mechums River in Albemarle to here."

Sandy raised an eyebrow, impressed with the learning, but countered, "The big problem was labor. Crozet lost most of his workers right away to a company in Cincinnati paying a dollar fifty a day. Virginia Central Railroad offered only a buck, two bits."

His tone revealed skepticism that such a rich company would not see the wisdom of keeping available workers for a little more a day.

"Then the Virginia Central brought in fardowners way over from Northern Ireland," he continued. "They lived mostly on the west side."

He chuckled at his next thought. "One day, fifty of them tried to vote democratic in a Waynesborough election. Let me tell you, these local folks didn't appreciate it. That Whig newspaper in Staunton said they came from the bowels of the earth to overwhelm the intelligent native-born citizens of Augusta. I don't know; I thought they were fine Presbyterians." He smiled warmly at the wit, but received a quizzical grin from Jud.

"Then the railroad brought in some Irish Catholics from County Cork," Sandy continued. "That started a riot. Broken bottles smashing heads. Splintered tent poles. Lost several days of work."

"How did they stop the rioting?" asked Jud, leaning forward again as he warmed to the action.

"Moved most of the Corkers to the east side," Sandy explained. "Then there was more trouble. One of them found a dead body, already rotting. He carried it back to his shanty and held a wake over it. Cholera broke out and killed a-hundred twenty-five workers. Thank goodness most of them were on the east side," Sandy said, still relieved.

"Inside the tunnel, more problems," he said, and Jud welcomed the continuing story to pass the time. "Crozet had to divert that Lithia spring right out the guts of the mountain. Imagine, Jud. All that black powder smoke, the hand-drilling and chipping, and water coming in on you constantly." Jud nodded, not able to get the full impact.

"Turned out rather good, though," Sandy reflected. "Crozet used a three-inch pipe—third of a mile long, it was—to run the water into a lemon-shaped pond on a terrace of the west slope. Built a park 'round it. And the overflow ran into the South River. Water on the other side went into Rockfish Run."

"Guess it finally worked out all right," said Jud, running his finger around the rim of his empty glass.

"Yeah. I'll never forget that Christmas day in fifty-six," Sandy said, smiling. "Little Gallaher, brother of that guy who owns the big Springdale house down by the river. They brought that skinny kid in to crawl through a small opening and make sure the work teams holed through all right. Came all the way in from both sides—sometimes only two or three feet a day—and were only a half inch off."

"The taverns opened up even on the holiday," he continued, enthusiastically. "The Irish stayed on the mountain; I hear some of the bosses took casks of liquor up there. But the important officials bought round after round down here. I declare, there were many, many more fireworks that night than any other Christmas anyone can remember." Jud tried to nod him on.

"There was still much work to do, though." Sandy's speech slowed again. "The tunnel wasn't finished for another year and a half. The first train through brought the mail, back in April of fifty eight."

"Why not just run the railroad over the mountain?" asked Jud.

Sandy reached for his glass to wet his throat before answering. It was empty. He thought about getting one of those new whiskey cocktails with a maraschino cherry. But he ordered two more sarsparillas. Jud nodded appreciatively.

"They did run a track over the mountain," Sandy said. "Completed it in 1854," said Sandy. "Only took Charlie Ellet seven months to do it.

"But I want to tell you." Sandy leaned forward. "It was one scary ride. They had to swing those trains 'round all those curves. And, when you got to the top, there was barely room for an engine with a few cars to pause on the narrow ridge before starting down into the valley."

Jud leaned forward, too, in anticipation. "They had to come down over two miles. Six miles per hour. A brake on every wheel," Sandy said. "You had to ride it to believe it. I heard figures like one foot down for every twenty-four feet of rail. It was just plain steep. Even worse on the east side."

"Sounds like the crew and passengers ought to be scared," Jud encouraged, bored with the technical details.

"The first passenger train was bought over the mountain by mules, hauling plenty of them dignitaries on a fancy passenger car behind a right glossy locomotive," Sandy obliged, but digressed. "Named the engine for the railroad president, they did. The F. Harris Jr."

"The train went on into Staunton. Then thirty-five people rode back across the mountain. There was supposed to be a big welcome on the other side, with banners and bands and everything."

Jud finally caught the excitement.

"The engineer decided to detach the passenger car at the top of the mountain and take the engine on in," continued Sandy. "On its way down, the coach's brakes failed. The brakeman jumped, but the others had a wild ride into Charlottesville, let me tell you. Several passengers were mildly injured. But that engineer got his. He saw the coach coming and jumped. He was run over when he fell back onto the tracks."

Jud stared at his grandfather, surprised at his harshness, then realized the old man merely thought the incident ironic.

"Well, did the route ever work?" he asked.

"Oh, yeah. There were four trips daily, most carrying forty, maybe fifty tons of freight and passengers," said Sandy. "Built a special water tank on the eastern slope to replenish the water for steam. Only once they didn't make it. The engine got caught in a snow drift up close to the top." Jud leaned back.

"There was too much maintenance, though, and always the chance of bad weather and runaways," Sandy said, concluding. "We were very glad when the tunnel was finished."

"Beautiful piece of work, the tunnel" said Jud. "Sometimes Sarah and I go up and walk a ways through it."

"You better be careful," said Sandy, a bit loudly. "One of those trains may come through ahead of schedule."

"Oh, Grandpa. It's all right. Many people do it," Jud reassured him. "We go up to the spring, relax by the pond and catch a ride back to Charlottesville for two bits."

"That's pretty cheap," allowed Sandy. "But one guy had an even better deal. You know that great gash on the mountain, kind of like a sandy scar in all that green up there?"

"Yes, sir," Jud replied. "Mr. Tollman said it's where they got the ballast for the tracks."

"That's true," Sandy said. "John Bell owned that mountain, but sold the title to it for a pass on the railroad for one year. The railroad got millions of tons of gravel. Bell only used the pass once."

Sandy slapped the table so hard, enjoying this tidbit, that the drink spilled. He leaped up quickly to save his new indigo britches. He grabbed the silver chain at the pant waist to look at the scrolled fob which lifted from his vest pocket.

"Time to go down and meet Margaret," he said, picking up his gray hat with the tiny cardinal feather in the satin band. Jud grabbed his military chapeau with the shiny black rim.

There was no mistaking Sandy's sister at the station. She was still stylish, just stepping down from the train in a close-waist dress of mauve silk trimmed in lace dyed to match. She wore buff leather gloves and ankle boots the color of doeskin. Her hair was perfectly coifed into two big rolls at the side of her head.

"Margaret, aren't you lovely," said Sandy.

"Not so bad yourself," she said, noticing the popular cream-colored wool shirt. "And this I—why it's Jud. Oh, so handsome you are in your uniform."

"Ma'am," he said, quickly taking off his hat to catch his aunt's peck on the cheek.

"We will see you tonight?" Sandy reminded him. "Ham biscuits, corn cakes, mince pie."

"I will be there."

"Might just be able to find that crock of blackberry preserves I packed somewhere in here," Margaret said as Jud turned to go. "I know how those cadets love them."

"Yes, ma'am," he saluted.

"I'm so glad you're here for awhile," said Sandy, picking up the bags and taking her arm as they walked down the street. "Jud and me were remi—thinking about the past while we waited for you. "Do you remember the old Gibbs Tavern that used to be down there?" he asked, pointing.

"Quite a place before the war," Margaret said. "As many as ten stage coaches coming in to change horses while the travelers had dinner. People from all over—Eastern Virginia, the Carolinas, even farther south. Most going West.

"I'm so glad we travel by train now," she continued. "I thought of you as we came through the tunnel," she said affectionately.

"Watch out," Sandy hollered at the peddler as his barrow caused nearly everyone on the street to take a wide berth. Some came back to look at the racks of skillets and tin cups, the spools of ribbon, and the brown glass bottles containing laudanum and various tinctures of herb in alcohol.

"Now you don't often see anything like that in Richmond," Margaret laughed.

"We're pretty plain and simple here," Sandy said a few hundred feet later as he opened the door to the small, white-washed clapboard house.

"Why, this is lovely," said Margaret as Sandy led her into the back bedroom.

"I tried to fix it up a little for you, since Jud lives in the new barracks at Fishburne now," Sandy said, looking around doubtfully at the plain iron bedstead, small chest of drawers, straight chair and writing table.

"These embroidered pillow shams are beautiful on this fine cotton spread," she said, unnecessarily smoothing the cover. "And a matching scarf on the chest."

"Maybe this will dress that up a little more," Sandy said, holding out a plain paper package tied with a red ribbon. "Happy Birthday."

"Oh, just like the ribbon on the cart," Margaret said, carefully opening the inside tissue.

"Oh," she said again with more emphasis, quickly unpinning a roll of hair to use the new brush with the tortoise shell handle."

Sandy returned to the room with a cup of tea in time to see Margaret unpack an onyx and pearl brooch, black shiny slippers, a pale pink evening dress and foamy white petticoats.

"Now I know I have to get us an invitation to the big soireé at Rose Hall Friday night," he said appreciatively. "William down at the bank says his wife never stops talking about the last party—especially the mahogany table covered with English china, silver flatware, and the beeswax candles in silver candlesticks." He rolled his eyes at the details. "Heard they serve ham and Tennessee liquor."

"I'm sure they absolutely must have a marble-topped sideboard with many welcoming decanters," Margaret teased, taking a sip of tea.

As she pulled out a less-formal, pale-yellow sweater and dark green skirt, Sandy said, "I was thinking we could go up to the spring on the mountain while you're here. Take a little picnic of fried chicken, potato salad, perhaps some vinegared cucumber slices.

"Maybe we can even walk a little along the rails in the tunnel."

Adelia was intrigued by the missing locket. However, she was a thorough researcher whose points of interest were exponentially expanded in many directions.

At first the library's local history room seemed to contain little information on Fairfax Hall—a few yearbooks and some pictures. Leafing through the yearbooks, Adelia had to agree with the Colonel that every picture should have a caption and every piece of text some real information. As a high school yearbook adviser, Adelia attended a workshop by this guru of championship yearbooks at the University of Oklahoma. It was hard to convince her students that such detail was necessary. However, Adelia mourned the lack of information in the "Fair Facts" and later the "Chain and Anchors" annuals of Fairfax. She did find a yearbook picture of her kitchen table—students sitting around it in the library.

Turning on her knees from replacing a book on the bottom shelf, Adelia spied the drawer label near the bottom of a filing cabinet on the opposite side of the room. "Waynesboro History." From its files, many hours of research were accomplished before she returned to reading specifically about the girls' prep school.

To a fairly new resident, Waynesboro seemed like a nondescript community, kind of flat like its expanse to the horizon. However, there were many nuggets of interest to her historical bent. She soon lost herself in the files, tunneling through them as Sandy had the train route.

Fairfax Hall was not originally in Waynesboro, she found. Neither was it—despite its Virginia colonial name—originally Fairfax. Perched on the bluff, the Hotel Brandon was the showplace of Basic City. There was no greater confirmation than a framed newspaper front page Adelia found on the wall in a back room of the Waynesboro Historical Museum.

Chapter 4

The inventor walked into an office on the first floor of the Jordan Building, one of several new structures in the fast-growing central business district of Basic City. His partners were waiting.

"Well, Jacob Reese. Good to see you. Nice trip down from Pittsburgh, I hope."

"Getting used to it, M. W. Good to see you again, Smittie, Jim, Charlie. How are you doing, L. G.?"

"Can't hardly keep up with it all, Jacob. We've grown to over twenty five hundred people. Factories and businesses everywhere. Carriages, freight cars, crates, sashes and blinds, pens and pencils, shirts, blankets, brooms, playing cards, cigars." He was breathless with the recitation. "And bricks—four brick plants. Nearly a hundred men making forty thousand bricks a day. Basic City is on the move."

Reese nodded and took a chair. "I can see that, L. G. When I picked up my mail last night, there was a letter from Ned Ingalls, you know, the president of the Chesapeake & Ohio Railroad. He said that Basic is the handsomest place he has ever seen for a city."

"The railroads have certainly done their part," Smittie said. "Sitting here on the Iron Cross hasn't hurt us at all. I hope the president of the Norfolk and Western is pleased, too. With the two railroads, we have ten passenger trains and fifty freight trains a day. People can get almost anywhere from here. And, we proudly ship our manufactured goods and the natural resources of the Shenandoah Valley up north."

"I knew this area had potential, gentlemen," said Reese. "I'm not sure I realized how much."

"I have to admit we were a bit skeptical of your, er, exuberance," said M. W. "I mean, 'after a tour of the whole south, no point offered the same advantages as this site?!'"

"Or was better adapted to making steel," said Reese. "Don't forget that," thundered the inventor of the Basic Process light-heartedly.

"I think Charlie said it best," M. W. suggested. "Where's that promotional booklet?"

He shuffled the pamphlet out of a stack of paper on the window sill and handed it to Charlie as he retrieved some glasses and a bottle of whiskey.

"On May 9th 1890, it was but a stretch of agricultural land, rolling picturesquely and skirted by a river," read Charlie. He flipped a page. "Located in the richest portion of the famous Shenandoah Valley, it has unlimited mineral and timber resources . . . ."

Another page. "Impure water, the parent of fevers, is unknown in the whole region. . . . Lithia Spring bubbles up spontaneously and fills a lake . . . sufficient for a town of thousands. . . . Its bottom throbs and palpitates with a force that produces one thousand gallons a minute. The air is full of balmy exhilarant. . . ."

"That was a particularly eloquent section," quipped L. G.

"Major Jed Hotchkiss, Stonewall Jackson's cartographer, says—um—The Blue Ridge region is the best sanitarium in the United States," the author finished.

"Now, you would not appreciate that endorsement so much, coming from the north and all," M. W. said to Reese. "However, you can find no better spokesman than the logistical genius of the man himself."

"Even a Yankee can appreciate the greatest coal, iron and limestone fields of America," replied Reese warmly. "And that Crimora mine, up the way. Supplies eighty percent of the total manganese consumption in the United States each year." He noted that the mine sent Pittsburgh twenty thousand tons in 1887—for steel, glass, ceramics, paints, tiles, bricks, and dry cell batteries.

"Ever the industrialist," said Jim. "Basic has grown from a hay rick, cow shed, little hotel, three houses and a hard cider store near the Waynesboro Junction depot. And he's still focused on the underground. Good for you, Jacob."

As M. W. distributed the glasses, the founders rose to their feet. "Here's to the Basic City Mining, Manufacturing and Land Company," he said. "To growth, expansion, and prosperity."

"Here, here." They raised their glasses, drank, and clapped each other on the back.

"How's that blast furnace coming along, Jacob?" L. G. asked as Reese prepared to leave. "One hundred tons isn't it, whatever that means. To you, I know, it's the key project in all this craziness." L. G. also appreciated its importance to Basic City. "Not just three-hundred-and-fifty more jobs, but more growth, more notoriety," he said aloud.

"Next on my list of things to work on after the big ball tonight," said Reese.

He went down the steps onto Augusta Avenue, stopping a minute to look at foundation work on the civic opera house. He considered going to his room at the Central Hotel next door but decided to take a walk along the dusty streets.

Raising a handkerchief to his face as a horse and rider went by, he sighed. Basic City was not Waynesborough, the older—some would say—more cultured city to the east, with its Valley Seminary for females, Fishburne Military School, Masonic building, opera house, and business complex. However, in its first year, Basic City grew from two buildings to one thousand, including a thirteen-story bank building.

"Still, it's essentially an industrial center fringed by picturesque cottages and a few grandiose villas," he mumbled aloud.

Most of the original twenty-five-foot lots sold for six hundred dollars in May, 1890, although Reese knew that one at Augusta and Fourth sold several times over for two thousand dollars. Others in what became the central business district brought one thousand to fifteen hundred dollars. In just seven months, the original six-hundred-dollar lots were selling for a thousand dollars. Reese was not sure of the going rate now, almost a year later.

Over breakfast this morning, he read an encouraging account in a regional valley periodical. "Manufactories going up on all sides, residences and buildings of every class completed and under construction," the article read. "This town has the appearance of a city, and the thriving, bustling, rushing air about the whole place is indicative of rapid progress in a material way."

"Oh, how I dread going through all that local mail gathering dust since I left for Pittsburgh," he thought. "It will take me hours."

Reese walked over to Fourth Street and turned right past the Basic City Bank with its arched Palladian windows to see the iron bridge across the N&W tracks. Sixty feet wide with a ten-foot sidewalk, it replaced the crossing which always seemed to be blocked by freight cars in the early days. The pedestrian bridge across the South River farther west on Third Street was prettier he knew from several overheard comments about the beautiful ornamental iron. He had not as yet strolled it himself.

Basic City was spreading out, from three thousand feet west of the South River eastward across the N&W tracks to where the Blue Ridge mountain slopes made construction impractical. Southward from the blast furnace site just north of Second Street to the lithia springs between Tenth and Twelfth.

There was enough water from the springs to supply Basic well into the future, with the added health advantages of lithium salts, iron and magnesia, which was a mild laxative and antacid. "Fortunate for me," thought Reese, patting his chest. "I've already spent a quarter of a million dollars on that furnace, and all we have so far is the foundation."

Still, an open hearth using basic refracting material, rather than the standard acid, removes sulphur and phosphorous and makes a cleaner slag—Reese mentally ticked off the features of his new process for which the town was named. "I have proved the process in models. Here is the opportunity to show it to the steel-making world." His languid steps became strides.

The industrialist turned south onto Commerce Street, still amazed at the potpourri of railroad tracks and sidings. Carts from many small businesses and wagons from coal yards and oil dealers abounded. Farther down, cattle would be complaining in the loading pens near Wenonah Hill, an odd geographical formation in the middle of flat land. Charlie said it was a moraine—a deposit of stone, gravel, and other earth materials left at the end of a long-ago glacier.

Approaching the spot where the railroads met at the fabled Iron Cross, Reese saw the new swiveled water pipe that let southbound steam locomotive engineers replenish their water supplies. Passengers, express shipments, and mail shared the brick platform. A sample case man—dressed in a cheap, fancy suit and spats—stood among the crates of corn, onions, potatoes, cabbage, eggs, and cans of milk. Absent today was the hurdy-gurdy man with monkey dressed in pillbox hat and red military coat with brass buttons. The salesman gazed up at, but probably did not see, the onion-shaped milk glass globes caressed by trim iron vines. They would light the platform for the late trains.

To the right was the Mountain View Hotel which offered amenities to tradesmen and general travelers. These included electric lights, steam heat, and porcelain bath fixtures bringing hot and cold lithia spring water. There was also a pool and billiard room. Outside, several chickens took dust baths in the middle of the road while others pecked at grain dropped from feedbags being carted from the siding to Coiner's Store.

The area had a number of bars, even the more numerous in Basic, Reese mused, because no saloons were allowed in Waynesborough. Soon, the Basic City fathers must deal with the lack of ordinances regulating bars, fireworks, guns, explosives, sanitation, and speed limits for wagons and trains. They had passed one law recently that animals running at large would be captured and sold at auction "for the good of the community."

Turning west, Reese headed up Fifth Street toward Augusta, wondering, as he made the turn toward his hotel, how the new *Basic City Advance* would cover the anniversary ball tonight. Reese visited with Publisher Lindsay awhile back at the offices near Wenonah Hill. He was careful not to laugh at J.H.'s prediction of six thousand weekly subscribers in three years.

As Reese entered the simple dining room of the hotel, he found it almost empty in mid-afternoon. A roasted chicken sandwich would tide him over until the banquet tonight and nourish his thoughts, he hoped, to pen a letter to his wife.

* * *

My Dearest Eliza,

It is hard to believe how much Basic City has grown in the last eighteen months. It's almost worth the kidding I take as a Yankee in this forever South. At least they don't call me a carpet-bagger. They are much too happy with the success here. Did you know that the Basic City Mining and Mineral Land Company was founded on the day that Jefferson Davis died? December 6, 1899. You remember, Davis was president of the Confederacy. In our meeting today, L. G. read the part of his promotional booklet, quoting the great review by General Stonewall Jackson's map maker. Stonewall still is the man here, you know.

Yesterday I visited with William Jefferson Loth (now there is a Southern name), owner of Waynesborough Stove Works They build two hundred stoves a day in six sizes—cook, portable range, heating, egg, cannon, and the Open Franklin with two-hole dwarf and fancy box. Do you prefer the wood, coal, gas or electric one, dear? Quite impressive. However I sincerely hope to find a similar manufacture in Pennsylvania.

Early today I visited the foundry built by the Rife and Schoppert Company in Waynesborough almost twenty years ago, just south now of our town line. They perfected hydraulic rams in several sizes, using water power to get more water from the South River up the city's substantial hills. The largest one is rated at forty-five to fifty gallons a minute. Someday we may use that power to get water from the lithia springs up the eastern slopes, particularly to the hotel.

A Boston investment firm recently issued a prospectus to further develop the Amazon Springs on the east side of Waynesborough. They say seven million gallons of pure water a day are expelled from the sandy spring bottom through small water/sand volcanoes. The prospectus brags about huge masses of water cress thriving there and how it may be harvested for distribution to better class restaurants along the east coast. They may build commercial water cress beds along the spring overflow.

The mineral spring waters are the important output, though. The hotels use them to attract guests from all over. They drink it and take baths in it, seeking cures for rheumatism, poor digestion, kidney and bladder troubles, female weakness, and general debility. (I pray I am not too frank.) Thanks to our great train service, people come from as far away as Philadelphia, New York, Baltimore, D.C., and Boston—more than 500 miles from there.

Elizabeth Tidwell

You must come down with me sometime to "take the cure." Not enough investors yet to build the Hotel Castalia. Its name comes from the fountain at the foot of Mount Parnassus in ancient Greece, the reputed abode of the gods. How is that for pretension? Some enthusiasts claim it will be the second Sarratoga of the U.S.

Instead, I shall take you to the Brunswick Inn. It opened in May, much grander than the preceding Ford Hotel purchased by the aforementioned Mr. Loth. The inn is renovated, expanded and named for the hometown of his new bride, New Brunswick, New Jersey. It has summer houses, dance pavilion, bowling alley, swimming pool, stables, gazebo, race track, and lithia spring houses. I believe it uses one of those hydraulic rams to get the lithia water into overhead tanks. And Mr. Loth told me that the stop watch was first used in America at the track in 1890.

The Brunswick's gardens and groves continue down to the South River—according to the advertisement—full of flowers and boxwood; apple, pear, mulberry, cherry, crabapple, walnut, hazelnut, and locust trees; red and black raspberry, white and black currant, and plum bushes. Can you imagine the delights of their summer dining room?

I toured the inn late last summer and admit to admiring its colonnade design. Its bricks are painted white, and it has dark green shutters and "continuous verandahs." I really must pronounce that last word for you when next we are together. No strokes of pen can do justice to the Southern pronouncement. The inn's eighteen rooms have Brussels and Moquette carpets and oak and cherry mirrors. I know you will love it.

Now I have gone on and on. And I have written far more about the wonders of Waynesborough than our own Basic enterprise. Somehow, I think I have bored you enough with our east side. And, most of it cannot compare, yet, with its neighbor.

However, tonight we celebrate Basic's crowning glory. I hear that six hundred invitations have been sent for the anniversary ball, including two hundred to the editorial fraternity of Virginia and nearby states. The manager, a Mr. Bowles, says there will be four hundred people there tonight.

Abide with me once again as I extol briefly on the virtues of our own Hotel Brandon, opened on Thanksgiving night, one year ago. It is said that it was designed by Stanford White, of the Washington Capitol extension and Madison Square Garden, but Architect William F. Poindexter is as yet wont to confirm that. As you may recall, the hotel is named for "Brandon-on-the-James," the birthplace of one of the builders, a Mr. Page.

It is so grand. Gabled entrance pavilion. Three-story towers with tent roofs on either end of the almost three-hundred-foot shingled, facade. Octagonal belvedere and cupola in center-roof. It would amaze and confound anywhere with its irregular symmetry and design idiosyncrasies. However, its perch on the bluff overlooking the city takes it beyond magnificence. How can anyone call it a mere railroad hotel?

Eighty guest rooms, it has, with furniture of carved oak. Guests hang their clothes on pretty little standing racks rather than hooks on the door. The corner rooms in the towers have Sixteenth-Century oak folding beds with matching drawers and mirrors. Each room has a steam radiator, although some guests still prefer the ones with fireplaces. Gas and receptacles for electric lights which are soon to be added. The bathrooms and toilet rooms on the third floor have hot and cold water. On the lowest level is a barber shop, billiard salon, and the office of the steam engineer who sees that all runs smoothly.

I have heard the hotel was built for forty-five thousand dollars, three times the cost of the Brunswick Inn. And another thirty thousand was spent on furniture, utilities, and decorations. But, my dear, I believe that it is worth it.

Oh, Eliza. You can scarce imagine the main floor. I dare say that all first-time visitors must stare in rapture at the magnificent foyer with its stately wood-paneled columns and broad fireplace with antique andirons. The ladies parlor has plush covered furniture of the most modern style and rich Brussels carpets. And the ladies exclaim over the curtains. The gentleman's reading room is in one of the tower corners and has an open wood fireplace flanked by radiators and a fine view out the windows.

Elizabeth Tidwell

Ah. But the dining room. It is immense, lighted by broad plate glass windows by day and gas chandeliers at night. Doors along the front wall open onto a long, arched porch. No verandah here. We call it a piazza in Basic. I can hardly wait to see the Brandon in all its finery tonight so that I can share even more of its lavish details with you.

You simply must come down with me next summer. We will stay at the Brandon, enjoy the baths, take long walks along the many wooded paths, and play croquet—oh, its a marvelous new craze here. We'll have dinner at the Brunswick on the lattice-lined verandah. And spend days seeing this wonderful new city that will make my name anew in the steel-family parlors of Pittsburgh. Promise me you will come, darling.

Oh, my dear. I must hurry to dress for the grand occasion up the bluff. I have ordered a carriage from Mr. Patterson's establishment. We shall go up over the Fourth Street bridge and but two or three squares, almost directly into the front carriage path of the hotel. Imagine the lines of swinging lanterns on all kinds of conveyances as their steeds prance up the lane to their turn on the porte-cochere.

Fondly, Jacob.

* * *

"No summer house gala of even the richest family of Newport, nor any Rhode Island casino, can match this," Reese thought as the carriage neared the Hotel Brandon's porte-cochere with its lattice frieze hung from shapely columnettes which also supported the ballustraded second floor balcony. "Quietly elegant."

Partygoers were anything but quiet as they almost ran through the open door. Welcomed by bright lights glimpsed through the three-part transom, they pressed to join the boisterous party seen through the sidelights and the now-open richly paneled door. Hotel guests with rooms front and center cast aside the louvers and shouted welcomes from the four windows of the massive gable's pediment. Others to the right called out from the arched porch near the tower. To the left, small, private parties occupied the two levels of the open air porch. Off the main entrance, guests of the ball, already with drinks in hand, gathered on the piazza enjoying the view of the city.

No one yet had made it to the belvedere and cupola on top. "Give them time," Reese thought. "May go up there myself."

Reese entered and, searching for the coat room, spied the wide central staircase. He almost laughed at the mass of swirling guests, some headed up, no doubt, to the comforts of the third floor, while others descended for more greetings and entertainments. It was hard to tell which direction was intended. Suddenly, he had a vision of feet, then bodies, breaking through the finely turned, narrow ballusters. The thought was interrupted by a young man coming to take his coat and hat. They soon lay atop a Jacqueminot red cape.

His way to the ballroom was blocked by many partiers, but most distinctly by a handsome lady in wine-colored silk, finely pleated across the bodice and moving in waves of material almost to the floor. "Oh, yes. Polly made it from a brand new pattern from *Harper's Bazaar*," said her conversational companion dressed in fashionable blue, close-waisted cashmere.

Sidestepping a bit, Reese almost made it down the hall before he was confronted with a young woman prancing to and fro among several eager suitors. She was dressed in some kind of rose-flowered material over a pale blue petticoat. "Satin," he thought.

The beautiful wood features of the dining room were almost hidden by two hundred guests, most at the enormous sideboards on either side of the room, spaced between the columns. The battle to the buffet was worth it. Oysters-Blue Point on the half shell, fish, mutton, broiled quail on toast, and tenderloin of beef on raised silver trays between candelabra, fronted by roasted red potatoes, carrots, pearl onions, turnips, and squash balls. Large tureens of mock turtle soup a la Hotel Brandon were on each end. And that was not the half of it. Reese sat for quite awhile, enjoying the repast and the lively music of the brass band from Charlottesville, which was crowded in the corner to the left of the fireplace.

Heading back for dessert and some more Mumm's champagne, he bumped into Montague Payne, the foreman who guided finishing touches on the hotel. "Getting enough to eat, Mr. Reese," he asked.

"Call me, Jacob—may I say Montague? I think this pudding with brandy sauce, may just about do it. You've done yourself proud,

Montague. I don't care what they call it—Queen Anne style or late Victorian. She's gorgeous."

"Thank you, sir. I am right proud of her, although she had her moments in those final days. It's a darn sight better than my previous work on barns, I will tell you. However, I am certainly glad to have a few less—well—ornate projects underway in Staunton."

"Bill Brown—I guess he goes by William Philip—did a nice job on the furnishings, too. Is it true that it all cost fifty thousand dollars? I have heard seventy-five thousand which, to tell the truth, seems a little closer."

"Not for me to tell, Mis, um, Jacob. There's a lot of money pouring into Basic right now."

"I was thinking about trying to find my way up to the Belve—"

"Oh, I can show you up," said Payne.

"No. Thank you. I think I will save it for another time," said Reese, grabbing a sprig of grapes. "I want my wife to come down from Pittsburgh this summer, and that will be a special treat for her."

Reese walked onto the piazza and across to the front entrance, past the winter-bare rhododendron, to avoid most of the crowd.

"Can I help you, sir?" asked a young man, somehow placid in the storm around him.

"Yes, thank you—uh, it is Mr. Huff is it not? Let you out from behind the desk tonight?"

"Yes, sir."

"Would you ask the young man to find my carriage? My driver is Sam from Mr. Patterson's. Then I will be obliged if you can find my coat and hat. The coat is a dark gray wool, and I left a light blue handkerchief hanging out the pocket. The silk matches the feather in the hat."

"Very good, sir. Right away."

Reese crossed the beautiful carpet, which swayed ever so slightly at each touch of the shoe, to get a good luck drink from the two-foot-high silver urn converted to a drinking fountain. It was inscribed "Manufactured for Hotel Brandon, 1890."

"It has been a very good year since then," he thought. And, I am going to need all the luck I can get in these next twelve months."

* * *

My Dearest Eliza,

    I had scarce the energy to climb the stairs to my room and loosen my waistcoat before sitting down, too very heavily, I fear, to write you a few words. I cannot even begin to tell you about the grandest of occasions. I shall save you copies of the press. I will try very hard to get a copy from Richmond; I believe they had a photographer there. You may even get a few words in the northern papers. I doubt that Basic will ever again see the likes of tonight.

    I took a good luck drink from the famous urn as I left. Through all the gaiety and rejoicing, I could not help but think of the tasks ahead and the inevitable sacrifices that must be made. In such a place as Basic, there is so much happening, and not.

    So many things can go wrong. Judge Gooch and Mr. Baumgardener are so excited about the car works here. The business will make fine coaches for the railroads and employ four hundred people. But, I wonder if prospects for investment are already dwindling. Mr. Booker has been keeping track of finances in New York and says some fear a monetary panic in the next few years.

    Forgive me for being so morose, my dear Eliza. Why, just tonight I was telling Mr. Montague Payne, the last foreman of the Brandon's construction, that I would save my trip to the belvedere on top and share the experience with you this summer.

    I wish now I had waited for tomorrow to open the business letter from Pittsburgh. I promised L. G. today that I would look into progress on the blast furnace in the morning. However, I opened the envelope just now, and more work on the furnace will have to wait. The gentlemen—I may not call them that much longer—at Bessemer Steel Company have initiated inquiries into the Basic Process patents. I fear there will be extended litigation.

    Still, just writing to you, my dear, lifts my spirits and fills my heart with desire to see you again. I shall be no more than a week, maybe nine to ten more days here. I must, of course, wait for coverage of the ball while attending to some odd bits of business and consulting with M. W. and the gents about the next steps for our grand Basic enterprise.

Elizabeth Tidwell

Not even the promise of the elegant day coach and stately Pullman sleeper service of the C&O's Fast-flying Virginia Vestibule Unlimited can begin to compare to my anticipation of our next moments together.

Fondly, Jacob.

Adelia returned to the library to retrieve more information about this town with such potential. She was sure the citizens of Waynesborough were impressed by the anniversary gala but still looked on Basic as hugely undeveloped. Afterall, Waynesborough had its own spectacular Brunswick Inn. And it was obvious from early newspaper accounts that the new city to the east was quite rough.

She thought back to her growing-up years in Dallas, Texas before the Metroplex. Fort Worth, thirty miles to the west, was not so affectionately called Cow Town by those east of the Trinity River.

Even now, Adelia went to professional meetings in Richmond, Virginia where moving the location south of the James caused a stir. Things were so "different" across the river, where people and businesses failed to join the metropolitan flair of the north and west sides. The same group of professionals would never join the chapter in the Shenandoah Valley. One group in Roanoke, in the New River Valley of Southwestern Virginia, was coming along though. Adelia enjoyed all three groups for different reasons.

She wondered whether the sophisticates of Waynesborough avoided the upstart Basic City, except for the saloons and opportunities for work in the large industrial area.

Chapter 5

"What's the matter, Jake? Sit down at the table here and have some cider. I've been washing and ironing all day, but I think the curtains look really nice. Do you?"

"They look great, Laura" he said absentmindedly, placing his twenty-two-inch baton on the table and grabbing a cookie. "You are looking at the one and only lawman in Basic City. They. . . ."

"What? What happened to Harry?" Laura looked over and nearly poured too much cider into an earthenware glass that matched the pitcher.

"Let him go. Said there wasn't enough for two men to do, and they had to cut the budget," her husband explained. "Closing the jail, too. Said it's seldom used except to accommodate tramps.

"I did get a promotion to sergeant, though," he said, although there was little excitement in his voice. "I get to pick up the strays, extinguish the street lamplights, and be the night watchman and general peace keeper at the train station."

"Is that all?" she teased, coming around the table to massage her husband's big shoulders.

Moaning contentedly, he said, "It's hard to believe things are so quiet. Why just a few months ago Harry and me used to chain men to the hitching rails outside the jail because it was overflowing from business at the five saloons along Commerce."

"I guess Patterson finally got it under control," Laura said. From a side table, she picked up a copy of the *Basic City Advance* dated July 1, 1897 and read from the mayor's annual report.

> It gives me great pleasure to be able to call
> your attention to the wonderful improvement in the
> morals of our town since the sale of intoxicating
> liquors has been prohibited. Ladies, gentlemen and
> children can now, day or night, travel our streets
> and not be confronted by drunken persons or by
> having to hear profane and indecent language.

"Well, they still have to watch out for the cow patties," Jake laughed. "Someday they will make them fence the pastures. Maybe when they pave the streets."

"Here's an interesting story," Laura said, looking at the bottom of the front page. "Do you remember Jud from down at the Presbyterian Church? Graduated from Fishburne. Had the Silver Creek Orchard." Jake tried to answer yes but failed to cut in.

"Shipped all those apples to England and ran the cider mill and cress beds on the farm," Laura continued. "He used to cut the cress and ship it to New York City." She emphasized each word, especially Nuuuuu.

"Yeah," said Jake tiredly. "Hasn't he been managing the vinegar company plant over on the west side of Waynesborough, along the C&O tracks."

"Right," she affirmed. "Says here he got caught in an oiling machine. Broke a shoulder and leg and fractured his pelvis. Oooh! Says the pressure was so great his eye balls were pushed to his cheeks. I could have done without that detail."

"I reckon Jud's wife will be making good use of the Fishburne Drug Store down at Main and Wayne," said Jake, taking another cookie and commenting about all the drugs, patent medicines, and medical supplies available there, along with tobacco, eyeglasses, and a good selection of books and magazines.

"I bet Sarah picks up some candy to see her through, maybe even a soda at the fountain while listening to that jukebox," Laura said. "She may decide she deserves to see the jeweler there after being home with Jud for a few weeks. You men are all crybabies when you are sick."

Jake put a thumb in his mouth and pulled it out to say, "What I really like about that store is the bulletin board out front. Good place to get some national news and sports scores."

"And you can watch Jim or Gleason fill up those cars at the gas pump. Now that is something," she said, walking over to pull the big wash tub out from under the sink. "How long you think before those au-to-mo-biles (she emphasized each syllable) replace the carriages carrying luggage between the trains and the Brandon and Brunswick, Jake?"

"I don't know," he replied. "Horses mean big business. Carriage houses, stables, hay and grain storage, grooming, vet care, drivers, harness and carriage repair. I imagine Mister Mayor's mule-drawn trolley will keep running between the two hotels, too, since the electric one never came to be."

"Hard to tell about anything right now with the recession and all," Laura complained. "Looks like we survived the Panic of 1893, but it really busted the Basic City Car Works. Sharon told me at quilting yesterday that Ben and Patrick planned to build ten buildings on the seven acres and over a mile of track. Jobs for three hundred people. Less than half of the building got done. Maybe seventy-five or a hundred people working there now."

"Yeah," Jake said. "The school desk factory closed last year. And the barrel and crate company only survived by making shipping containers for apples. The Match factory closed even earlier, in ninety-five."

His chuckle startled Laura. "A momentous year that was," Jake said. "Everyone got so excited about the oil well that spring. "Never did get any oil, but they struck some fine water six hundred feet down."

He continued to recite the year's adventures as if preferring the good old days. "Harry and I got to arrest the boys for racing carriages down Augusta. You and me helped organize the folks to plant those two hundred trees. And I had to round up all the men to pick up that rock slide from the railroad cut. You and the ladies sure rewarded us with some fine pies for that."

Laura picked some ragged lint out of the tub. "I miss the Paper Fabrique Company. Just the name. And what beautiful playing cards and paper they made," she sighed. "I have a few sheets left. Too bad they changed to a grist mill and shirt factory.

"Martha said out at the fence today that she heard the Page Cigar Factory is going under," she continued. "I wonder where the Basic Lodge of the Odd fellows will meet if they lose that building. Charlie will not be happy."

"I would miss those cigars." Jake pulled two fingers from against his mouth and tilted his head back to blow smoke rings of imagination. "I like the Belle Brandon cigars but prefer the Iron Cross brand."

"Anyway, looks like Waynesborough is making a fast recovery from the big fire last year," said Laura. "Burned the whole block—bank, newspaper, development company, and the business college. But new buildings are going up. Little John got a job in the construction."

"I ran all the way across the river that night," Jake leaned his chair back on two legs and boasted. "Saw the flames over the knitting factory from down on the N&W tracks. I'll never forget Chief Jesser and his men trying to fight those soaring flames with that little hose mounted on the spoke between those great wooden wheels. At least it was at the end of winter so the men didn't roast alive."

"That's so true," Laura agreed. "Just a month later—for three days!—we had that early heat wave. Whooo!" She waved her hand vigorously back and forth. "It was ninety-three, ninety four in the shade."

Looking up at the unexpected breeze, Jake said, "What are you making?"

"Two batches of soap, if I can find the receipt. All the boiling and skimming and boiling and tipping this is going to take. My birthday is coming. I sure would like to have some of that Betsey Bell soap from Lyndhurst. I would smell so sweet."

"You smell just fine," he said reaching to grab her. She deftly escaped and went over to get the soda ash.

"Some time I just want to get all pretty and go over to Waynesborough, maybe Staunton."

"Oh, I think we can avoid Staunton," said Jake. "The flood water is probably still going down over there. Water up to your waist last fall."

"Oh, Jake, you're so funny. Everybody knows they had to bring all the run off over to Waynesborough last winter to flood the new ice skating rink."

"Yeah. So we could use our counterfeit nickels to get in." Jake said, marveling again at the criminals' long success.

"At least there are things to do in Waynesborough," Laura sighed.

"Wait a minute, Laura. You went down on our fair, dusty Augusta Street a couple of years ago," Jake mocked. "Professor Chew gave us all lessons on how to ride those new bikes, with the front and back wheels the same size."

"How could I forget?" She enjoyed the banter. "But Waynesborough. The dress stores...."

"The rooster from Hampton," Jake laughed. "Nothing like a good fighting cock to take care of the upstart in town. Now all the roosters on Chestnut Street can strut their stuff."

"Oh, you. What about the music concerts, the opera?" Laura asked. "Do you think we'll ever get our opera house built?"

"J.T. Lighner's not going to give up that dream, Laura. Brick and granite, steam heated, fireproof, lighted by electricity...."

"Mother always loved to describe the designs she saw. Let me recite quite properly," Laura said with a sophisticated tone. "The walls artistically frescoed in ancient classic design and devices on the outside denoting music, art and drama to illustrate in tasteful style the uses to which this beautiful temple will be dedicated."

"Now isn't that lyrical," teased Jake.

Laura hit him lightly with a scraper. "Where did those instructions get to?"

"I'll tell you the instructions I need," said Jake with just a hint of hoarseness. "A receipt for something or other and bad colds in throats. Here it is," he said, fishing a pink-stained sheet out from under some books and a water bottle. "Diptha . . . How do you pronounce it?"

"Dip-there-e-ah," Laura coached.

"Well I'm working on the bad cold in the throat," Jake warned and read, "Now you

>Take one 4th teaspoonful Cianpepper
>1 teaspoonful common table salt
>1 pint boiling water
>Add vinegar til write sour
>Add honeye or sugar either will do till
>rite sweet

"The honey is important, Honey!"

>Now put in bottles or cans make air tite
>Now is ready for youse. Shake well
>before youseing
>Directions for youseing the above made
>syrup:

>For adults take one table spoonful
>For children take one teaspoonful
>If the case is a bad one, it may be
>repeatet oftener.

"Maybe I will just take the honey licked from your lips."

"Oh, Jake. Settle down. I still have some magic elixir from last year," Laura said. "Now come down to the cellar and help me get the grease for this soap. If I carry twenty-six pounds up those steps by myself, I will be the one needing some healing spirits."

Adelia was spending a rare evening off sitting on the flagpole terrace wall, idly watching Mollie run barely into and out of the pasture. Although she often practiced selective hearing, the cocker would eventually get tired of chasing squirrel trails and respond to a call to go in.

A car coming up the drive, however, made Adelia grab the leash and frantically look for the dog who had no traffic sense whatsoever. The old man parked in a traditional space this time and slowly eased his way out of the Buick, giving a cheery hello as Adelia clicked the catch on Mollie's collar.

"Nice evening," he said.

Adelia nodded, still not sure of this mystery man.

"All settled in?"

"Yes. And I've spent some time exploring. It's an interesting place," she responded brusquely. "You'll have to come back some time, earlier. Maybe I could show you around. The kids, you know. Just settling down. And the neighbors in the back building are wary of anyone roaming around after dark."

"Of course. I see," he said, leaning against the car and looking up to the cupola. "I don't know what attracts me here. I don't have any connection with the place."

"Well, it's pretty, uh, imposing. You can't say that about many things in this area other than the mountains themselves," Adelia said, shifting her weight to the right foot and letting Mollie run out a bit on the retractable leash. "By the way, I've been doing some research on this place. I haven't found anything about a locket. Do you have any information about when it was lost? By whom?"

"Well, let's see. There was a big wedding," he said, looking at Adelia and back to the building. "Don't know when, maybe the early nineteen hundreds. To tell you the truth, I don't even remember why I think that," he said, shrugging.

"The timing sounds about right. This was a grand hotel once," Adelia said. "I can't imagine a large wedding during its years as a girls' school from what I know of the layout now."

He stumbled as he pushed away from the car but waved off Adelia's motion to help.

"You keep on looking, and I'll try to remember where I ran across this little . . . mystery," he chuckled. "Good night."

Adelia thought of the man again the next afternoon as she took old Highway 250 into Charlottesville for her late work shift at Kinko's. He talked once about some connection to the University of Virginia.

Slowing behind backed-up traffic, she looked to the left at the white fence surrounding an apparently large estate. "Mirador," a historical marker read, just close enough to see that, but not the description under it. Now, where had she seen that name?

Chapter 6

"Halloo, Edwin. What's all the bother?" George said, greeting the Hotel Brandon manager across the reception counter. "I haven't seen this much commotion since I got the steamer up to full speed and scattered all the horses on Augusta."

"Say, I hear you sold Virginia's first. Sold 'THE Dawson Automobile' to Luther and John Clarke. That's too bad, George." Edwin noticed the hotel's barber was still generous with the after shave.

"Had to do it. Couldn't get a loan for the second one. And everyone was always complaining about runaways and dangers to the children—"

"Hey, young man," Edwin shouted into the lobby. "Watch where you're swinging that board. If you're not careful, we'll have to call Doc Griffith up from the railroad office to patch heads."

Turning back to face Waynesborough's motorcar designer, Edwin said, "Reckon he would be driving that new car. Traded in his buggy a couple of months ago. Goes around singing, 'In my merrie Oldsmobile'.

"Nobody complains about his driving. Hard to complain about that man," he said with admiration.

"That's the truth," affirmed George. "No vices for him. You'd have to put out that cigar if he comes here, Edwin," he stressed, waving away the smoke wafting toward his face. "Sumpter never has allowed smoking in his home or office. I bet not in his car either."

"Doesn't like liquor traffic much either, eh George," Edwin said leaning over the counter as if it were a secret. "Do you remember when he horsewhipped that saloon keeper on Commerce? The fine people down the hill at Basic Methodist Church must be right proud."

"Probably," allowed George, "but I'm not so sure they're happy about all the new town ordinances this month. Only milk cows and heifers can run at large, and they can't wear cowbells. And, I know for sure the minister is upset about allowing liquor again, especially to minors—even with permission."

"But we've needed some of those laws a long time," Edwin said. "Many of our guests complain about smells from the privies and the hog pens and slaughterhouses. Ruins a fine walk."

"Personally, I'm glad to see the bans on smoking in stables and open fires near buildings," said George. "Why, look at Lambert's lumber yard and Luther's hay and grain store. And, Waynesborough just had another big fire that took out a whole block. Even damaged the firehouse."

"I hear Cecil Wright got home after fighting that fire and removed his raincoat—totally covered in ice it was. Stood it upright on the back porch to thaw while he slept!" Edwin guffawed.

"Do not doubt it a bit." George grinned. "So what's going on here? Are you rebuilding?"

"Just about, George. A guy from across the mountain rented the whole hotel for three days to marry off his daughter, Phyllis, to some guy from New York. Says the Brandon is the perfect place.

"Close to the railroads so the groom's guests can bring their special rail coaches down from up north," he explained with mock haughtiness. "And this guy's family and friends can come in from Richmond and Lynchburg and Danville. Of course he needed to make a few changes. And, we were already renovating upstairs."

"Who is this guy?" asked George. "He must be rich."

"I guess so. It's Chiswell Dabney Langhorne. 'Chillie,' they call him," replied Edwin. "Bought that big estate, Mirador, over toward Charlottesville a few years back. Made all his money working with the railroad barons from the north after the War Between the States."

Elizabeth Tidwell

This time he caught George's angry look and blew the great puff of smoke to the inside of the office.

"I guess some people really resent him," Edwin continued. "But his family went through hell in Richmond during the war. Times were not much better for them in Danville, I hear."

"Wait," said George. "Wasn't he the fellow whose daughter married that advertisement illustrator, Charles, er Dana, Gibson, I think?"

"That's the one," Edwin affirmed. "Irene became the Gibson Girl model. Makes all the rotos. That cute little upturned nose, very slender waist." Edwin pulled his hands around in curves. "And just a shade of disdain. The new emancipated woman."

"More like a princess," George said appreciatively.

"Yes sir," Edwin agreed. "Passive and golden for her royal wedding of north and south in Richmond a few years ago."

"The other daughters are real—shall we say—cultured, too, as I recall," said George. "Ride to the hounds. Beautiful debutantes. Always making the press at some horse show or society event."

"You got it. And Phyllis is marrying Reginald Phillip Brooks," Edwin said in a tone deep from his nasal passage. "A Harvard man. New York Knickerbocker and Racquet Club. Yachting. Supposed to be fifteen groomsmen from college and sixty or so other close friends and family members arriving this evening on the Fast Flying Virginian."

"That crowd ought to keep Pattie's fellows busy getting their trunks up the hill from the station," George chuckled, flipping the edge of a registration card.

"Mr. Langhorne says Phyllis and her older sister, Nancy, are coming over early tomorrow morning in a carriage," Edwin added.

"Followed by a long train of wagons, no doubt."

"I don't know, George. Mr. Langhorne's been over so often to oversee this set up, I think most of the wedding things must already be tucked away upstairs. We put the bride down in the room near the north turret. That way she'll be away from the groom and his entourage."

"I'm sure Mr. Langhorne will see that the fellows are otherwise occupied when the ladies arrive," said George. "If they're not still abed after seeing the local sights down on Commerce, if you know what I mean." He winked.

"Chillie will show them a good time for sure," Edwin agreed, slipping into the familiar. "He's quite a character. Before railroading, he was a tobacco auctioneer. Invented his own gobbler language, he calls it. Did a bit of it for me yesterday. Extraordinary."

"Well, I must be going, Edwin." George turned to the coat rack next to the lobby railing across the hall. "I don't suppose the public is invited to this soireé?"

"Oh, my, no. It's to be the meeting of the dashing Newport set with the least reconstructed family of Virginia on sacred southern soil," Edwin said with the appropriate amount of pomposity, remembering Chillie's description. "Mr. Langhorne says he was disappointed with Nancy's wedding. I don't think this one will be a problem."

"It looks like this may rival the anniversary ball," Edwin said with a quick wave goodbye. "Sorry I'm going to miss it."

* * *

"Everything ready for the bride, Mary?"

"Just taking the last of the towels up now, Mr. Goode. The gents are sleeping in. From what Harold said, I better make sure all their things made it at least to their doors and out of sight of the ladies' end. Must have enjoyed the atmosphere down at the Mountain View, er Belmont, last night. I still can't get used to that new name."

"Come right back down, Mary, and bring Esther and Tim and anyone else you can find. Mr. Langhorne is expecting three cart loads of chrysanthemums this morning."

"Whoo-eee! Miss Phyllis will get a garden wedding after all," Mary said, almost prancing toward the back stairs.

* * *

"Well, this is . . . something," Nancy said, stepping out of the carriage and making a slow turn to take in the porte-cochere and the arcaded porch.

Elizabeth Tidwell

"It certainly is not The White, Nance. I wish we could have the wedding there," Phyllis complained. "We had such a grand time each summer flirting and dancing."

"I guess Daddy's right though," Nancy said. "This is more convenient for everyone to get here. And, he could not have rented out the hotel at White Sulphur Springs. He'll make it grand here."

"I guess Reggie will think it good enough; down home provincial he'll call it. I don't know about his mother," Phyllis said doubtfully.

"Nanaire will think it's splendid and will be ever the perfect hostess," Nancy said encouragingly. "Mother's Irish blue eyes and keen wit will charm everyone. Let's go in and see what Chillie has been up to."

"Come on girls," Buck said, grabbing their arms as they came through the doors. "No stopping and gawking. Daddy wants you hidden away before the boys get about."

"Did Reggie get in all right? What does he think? I bet he's absolutely bored."

"I really don't think so, Phyl. And Harry and Keene are taking all the fellows riding this morning after a bite down at the station. Daddy says they serve great eggs and turkey hash."

* * *

Entering the room, Nancy said, "Well, this is . . . ."

"Something," finished Phyllis with a resigned chuckle. "Look at that hole up there in the corner, the curtains are blowing all over, the trunks are everywhere. . . ."

"Oh, it's so grand, Phyllis," said Nora, coming through the door with a small bag. "Old John said you left this in the carriage. He was quite stern you know," she added, holding it out for emphasis.

"You should come see the attic. There's a cupola on top, and you get a wonderful view of the mountains. Not much to see out there though," the youngest sister said, pointing to the west. "Bunch of train tracks and puffing smokestacks. Wish I could go riding with the boys."

"You better go see if you can help Nanaire or Chillie, you little sprite," said Nancy with a touch of exasperation.

Phyllis skirted a trunk and took a long look at the hole before going over to gaze out the window. The hole's ragged edges seemed to spread farther apart the longer she stared.

"The view is pretty though," she said aloud, shaking off the sadness. "I bet there are some great riding trails over there in the woods and back up into the mountains."

"Always the horsewoman," Nancy said. "The best of your generation at riding to the hounds according to that paper in Connecticut last month."

"Not so bad yourself, Nance," Phyllis rejoined. "However, you really take the trophy with your comic wit and mimicry."

"Now see here, Miz Phyllis and Miz Nancy," the older sister intoned in a high voice with hands on hips. "You girls need to be out doing somethin'. You are wastin' the morning."

"Yes, Auntie Liza. Oops! Yes, ma'am, Miz Pie. Need a light for your pipe?" Phyllis said gaily but her smile quickly faded. "I would be happy to spend the morning polishing saddles and harnesses in the barn."

"Reggie would not much appreciate your achieving the resulting aromas for this occasion, Phyl," Nancy admonished. "Chillie would probably threaten you with his eau de cologne."

"I'm going to miss Auntie Liza, Nance. And Auntie Ann, and Fannie. But especially Auntie Liza,"

"We all do, Phyllis. She's been the Mirador mammy for a long time. And she took care of Lizzie growing up in Danville." Nancy sighed. "I wish I could find someone like her for Bobbie. Three years old and already cock of the walk. Auntie Liza will have her hands full with him today."

"Buck said she has borrowed this huge copper kettle from a Mr. Rife and is going to be out back with all the children making apple butter," Phyllis said. "Daddy says it's a tradition around here, according to the hotel manager. Not at weddings, just any bright November day."

"Well, I hope she started early," Nancy said. "Blanche told me once that it takes all day. Said she was ready to get back to scrubbing the kitchen after stirring those apple sections and cider from morning to supper. In a figure eight pattern," she emphasized. "Blanche explained it to me in great detail." She drew out the "great" to three syllables, while rolling her eyes.

"Daddy says Mr. Rife's kettle comes with a custom-made paddle, long enough so you can stand back from the fire." Phyllis was relieved at that, but joked, "I hope they keep the children well back; they might ruin the flavor if they fell in."

"If they're as dirty as we were," Nancy agreed.

"Ah, the days of cartwheels, and whistling through our fingers and tap dancing with blind little Willie. Those were the days"— Phyllis paused remembering.—"Before we donned our young women's yashmak veils against the sun." She played the sophisticate. "They're okay for riding. But I think my tennis and squash games— I know my shooting—would be better without one."

"There is so much land to ride at Mirador," reflected Nancy. "Do you remember the first time we saw it, Phyl?"

"I remember eight of us piled on the platform at Greenwood Station with all the trunks," she replied. "And there must have been five or six dogs."

"And the goat," laughed Nancy. "Those beautiful carriage horses wanted to bolt from all the ruckus, but yellow John held them tight."

"It was hard to believe the change in Daddy, the change in our lives, when he bought Mirador," Phyllis said softly. "I was so happy to leave Danville, Nance. It was so dreary."

Nancy agreed. "Mother loves the gardens and has the scenery to paint those watercolors. Even did some scenes in needlepoint. Still does."

"Daddy began to sing the old plantation songs again and invited the old blacks in to fiddle and play the banjo," Phyllis said wistfully. "We danced and all sang close harmony, except you, Nance. Absolutely no sense of tone. But you and Daddy led us in some fearsome games."

"We sure did," said Nancy. "Several years ago, Fannie told me that she once ran to Auntie Ann saying how cruel we were being with our game of Truth. 'Horrible sounds of weeping coming from the parlor'," Nancy mocked with a fearful, trembling voice. "Auntie Ann told her to go back and listen for the peals of laughter."

"We were so close then, Nancy," Phyllis said, lost in melancholy. "I don't know how we keep it together now. Nora ever the totally irresponsible dream child, and Harry always off spreeing in the mountains. Irene with Dana on their grand tours of Europe, and you and Robert traveling all over New England." She sighed so heavily, Nancy thought she was going to cry.

"The only one who stays home is Lizzie, over there in Richmond with all that solemn Victorian decorating and endless talk of genealogy," Phyllis continued.

"Over fine mint juleps," Nancy proclaimed lightly.

"Oh, I miss her, Nancy."

"Well you can't expect her to come all the way over here with that great round of pregnancy," Nancy teased sternly. "I hope it's a girl."

"She and Moncure are caught forever in the shadow of reconstruction over there in Richmond," said Phyllis morosely. "All their lives it's been that way. She born not two years after the war, and Monnie at the beginning of it. Their house was built out of the rubble," she stressed.

"But they choose to stay, Phyllis," Nancy admonished. "There's a shabbiness there. But there's also a close knit pride, where everybody knows their neighbors for blocks around. Lizzie loves the social Sundays on the porch after church." She waved her hand daintily for effect. "They read French memoirs of the seventeenth and eighteenth centuries."

"Why, we may have all been the same if Daddy had not run into that guy from the Chesapeake and Ohio who took pity on the starving little man who wanted to build railroads," Phyllis said gratefully. "At least, that's the way Mother tells it."

"Oh, Phyllis, you are always so introspective—sensitive and melancholy, Chillie says."

"And, you, Nancy, are so witty—compelling and flamboyant, Daddy calls it."

Their pillow fight—running in and out around the trunks—lasted fifteen minutes, until Nanaire set a tray of tiny sandwiches down on a trunk heavily and sighed as the sisters collapsed on low couches among a virtual storm of feathers.

"You better start getting your things out," their mother said. "The dresses are in the next room. Miss Emily made sure they were pressed earlier.

"I checked on the others girls," she added. "I had to pull Lena and Dora off the little patio on the porte-cochere roof. They were waving wildly as the boys pranced their horses by a little while ago. You two could not hear it for all the ruckus in here, thank the Lord."

"Is Mrs. Brooks all right, Mother?"

"She is just fine and dandy, Phyllis. I gave her a small bottle of mercury and a turkey feather to work on the bedbugs."

"Oh, mother . . . ."

"She's fine, Phyllis." Nanaire said the words slowly and forcefully. "I don't know whether Mr. Brooks will ever be the same, though, after several hours with your father and his stories," she said, pausing only seconds, "including the one about buying all the left-footed shoe samples from that salesman on the train as we were coming back from the World's Fair in Chicago." She shook her head.

"I don't know whether Mr. Brooks was more shaken by the stories or from Chillie's bossing him and the workmen around to get everything just right downstairs," she continued. "Everyone has to do his part. You know your father."

"It's so beautiful, Phyllis. You're going to love it." Nanaire gave her a hug. "Don't forget to check your traveling trunk to make sure you have everything."

* * *

"Pull it tighter, Nancy," Phyllis said as she used dogwood twigs to brighten her teeth. "I will never get into that gown. Where are my shoes? Where are the gloves?"

"Settle down, Phyl," Nancy commanded, slipping the petti-coat over her head and then the white satin gown trimmed in lace. "You are so very beautiful," she murmured.

"Not so bad yourself," Phyllis said, putting on dainty pearl earrings. "That blue chiffon is very becoming."

"Here are your shoes. Step right in. And I put your gloves over there on the trunk. What a riot," Nancy said, looking around at the towels, glove boxes, shoe bags and half-open trunks.

Memories Will Always Linger

"Where is that locket?" asked Phyllis suddenly, looking around at the confusion. "Mother said a strange rider brought it up on the porch at Mirador just before she locked the trunk Tuesday. I hadn't thought about it until just now, but I want to see who sent it. Maybe I'm supposed to wear it."

"Where is it supposed to be? Which trunk?" queried Nancy.

"Mother said it was in the blue one in the top drawer, no the second one down, on the right under the pink stole."

"Here it is," Nancy exclaimed brightly. "Ooof, it's stuck. Oh, no."

"What happened? Phyllis gasped, turning quickly from putting the final touches on her hair, swirled around the diamond crescent."

"I don't know where it is, Phyl. The chain caught on the edge of the drawer. And I pulled, and it just flew off," Nancy apologized. "We'll never find it in all this mess. Nanaire will be here any minute."

"We have to find it! It may be from Daddy. Dana said one of the New York fashion firms was sending something. Or maybe it's from Reggie. Reggie," she nearly screamed. "What will they say if I'm not wearing it!"

"Calm down, Phyllis," called Nanaire. "They'll hear you downstairs."

"But Nancy lost the locket, Mother. What will Reggie say?"

"Tell him you wanted to wear this beautiful rope of pearls he gave you for your birthday," she said, pulling them out of a brown trunk. "They go beautifully with the earclips."

* * *

As Phyllis climbed the four steps to the middle of the hall, she heard the orchestra. Her mother was at the top of the stairs, giving last minute instructions to the bridesmaids, who began their descent in white chiffon and lace and white picture hats. Nanaire followed in an ankle length green velvet gown. As Phyllis met Chillie at the top of the stairs, Nancy stepped off the middle landing.

"Let's go, Phyllis," urged Chillie, who had traded his ubiquitous Panama hat for a bowler. Not even the mustache was drooping. As they paused at the landing, Phyllis gasped at the transformation of the room.

Chillie said, "See I told you it would be grand. You're the perfect final touch. You've never looked prettier, except maybe riding bareback over those snake fences."

"Oh, Daddy," Phyllis groaned, but turned to give him a peck on the cheek.

There were more than a few whistles from the men, and shushes from the women, as father and daughter descended the staircase into a forest of fall blooms, meeting Reggie at the foot of the stairs. Giant balls of white chrysanthemums were in every corner and all strategic locations.

Father and mother led the bride and groom toward the platform at the rear of the hotel lobby, then stepped back as the couple joined barely half of the bridesmaids and groomsmen at the altar. There, they were surrounded by potted plants and the rest of the bridal retinue now encircling the space. Phyllis looked up shyly at Reggie and saw a huge chrysanthemum ball hanging overhead.

Guests were everywhere, Phyllis heard later. She did not remember much about the ceremony. Over three-hundred-fifty guests pouring down corridors on either side of the lobby, the in-laws tucked under the stairway, and more guests flowing out onto the entry porch. The mid-November early afternoon was just cold enough that no one overheated in the crowded room. And the twenty or so guests relegated to the porch did not freeze. However, all were pleased to quickly follow the couple to the ballroom reception after the short ceremony.

"I have seen you at the most glamorous balls, the finest hunt breakfasts, beautifully astride the most handsome horse, and relaxing aboard the grandest yachts," Reggie whispered as they walked into another forest—of mahogany pillars and paneling, and even more chrysanthemums. "But nothing will ever compare to this."

"I should not think so, Rege Pege," Phyllis cooed. "But we have the rest of our lives for you to try."

"There's not any way I can compete with that, Dear Old Pills." He pointed.

Phyllis had to stand on tiptoes to see over the plants to a forty-two-foot round table, covered with roses and dozens of silver bouquet holders. In the middle was an enormous silver cup from the Harvard Porcellean Club.

"Oh, my," she gasped.

"Come on children. It will take some of these people hours to find their place cards, and they are all starving," grinned Chillie, leading the way to the table side just left of the open hearth fireplace, with a view of the thirty-piece orchestra across the room. "They seem like a half-mile away," thought Phyllis.

John Jacob Astor sat between Nanaire and Nancy. Payne Whitney next to Nora. Stanford White already was engaged in a discussion with Irene, probably about the hotel's design or the house he built for her and Dana in New York.

As the last of the guests found their places at the table, Phyllis and Reggie led the way to one of two lengthy, mirrored buffets. "Chillie told me the shellfish, spot, and shad are from Baltimore," whispered Reggie in her ear.

"Well, the ham, jowl, corn pone, and black-eyed peas are from Virginia," Phyllis tittered. "And that is Maria's turnip salad. And, over there, Uncle Richard's spareribs."

"It will take Mother and Father weeks to recover from this," Reggie said with a mock groan.

"Wait until a few toasts of the garlic sherry," Phyllis giggled. "I'll have Harry see that some laudanum gets to their rooms."

It seemed to Phyllis that the dining and toasts went on for hours. And they had. "I wonder when the orchestra will run out of tunes," she mused tiredly.

On cue, the instruments softened and a haunting voice began to sing the old song

> I'm going home to Dixie
> I'm going where the orange
> blossoms grow. . . .

Phyllis was not the only one in tears as Chillie finished, standing with Panama hat in hand, large gold cigar cutter hanging from his watch chain, and gold snake rink on his upraised left hand. Mr. Brooks led the wave of applause.

* * *

As Phyllis and Reggie left the ballroom to change, they saw Keene and Buck in the glow of gaslights at the front door with the traveling trunks. And they ran into little Bobbie and several friends at the foot of the stairs.

"We made apple butter and put it on hot bread right out of the oven," Bobby said, swinging his hand with the imaginary knife against a pretend slice in the other.

"That I can see," Reggie said, looking at the smears and crumbs on the happy faces, and checking his Rockford pocket watch with its golden hands and ivory case.

"I'll look forward to having some of your butter at Mirador this Christmas when we get back from Aiken in South Carolina," said Phyllis.

"Why would you be aching in South Carolina," Little Todd quizzed, as Chillie's booming voice invited all within its range to Mirador the next day to view the wedding gifts and have some more fine southern cooking.

"Especially the press," he bellowed.

* * *

The railroad platform was full of people the next morning—including a photographer and several young men with paper pads and pencils—waiting to catch the train to Greenwood Station.

Yellow John and the Langhorne sons took many of the traveling items and almost all the staff and children back to Mirador in several wagons the night before. Chillie knew that Auntie Ann and Miss Emily had awakened Fanny, Blanche, Richard, and the others from their clapboard cottages at dawn to make everything ready.

Auntie Liza would get up in her own time, but in plenty of it, to see that everything was just right. And to give a last lecture to the children to mind their manners. After the first welcoming, she would take them out to the nursery. Later they would play inside the white picket fence, dashing along the herring-bone brick paths and between the square beds, devoid of Nanaire's prized flowers and most of the vegetables this time of year.

Chillie was sorry his guests would not see the orange trumpet vines below the back porch on the white-washed smokehouse. Here the hams hung and cured for two years.

As the train got underway with a series of short jerks, he started moving through the two special coaches to find Mr. and Mrs. Brooks. "They're not here, Chillie," said Nanaire. "I believe they've had enough southern hospitality for a long time. They'll see the gifts at Phyllis and Reggie's later."

Within minutes, the train entered the Rockfish tunnel. Chillie wondered if it was still the longest in the world. After a few minutes of muted sunlight on the other side, they approached the Newton tunnel.

"This is the earliest mountain tunnel in America," Chillie told the press man seated across the aisle. "Built by Colonel Crozet who built roads across the Alps for Napoleon. It comes out right above my place, Mirador."

Buck, Harry and Keene each drove a wagon to the station to meet the train. The brothers courteously helped the few ladies to seats on hay bales covered with oil cloth. Many of the men got a better whiff of country aroma sitting on the fresh-hay-covered floors of the simple conveyances. On the two-mile trip to the house, Keene indicated the Humpback formation of the Blue Ridge Mountains and other points of interest to his guests. Chillie entertained his group with plantation songs and persuaded a few to join in.

Harry's wagon crossed the stream and turned left into Mirador's gate. He waited for Buck to clear the path ahead before driving to the top of the hill and turning through the ivy-covered arch. Ahead was the square red brick house with green shutters framing Georgian windows, built in 1832. His father added low wings with long porches on either side just after its purchase sixty years later.

Chillie jumped down from Buck's wagon and was met affectionately by Bob, the aging pointer. Young Tim quickly whisked him way as Chillie directed Harry to pull the wagon around the mosaic gravel circle so that guests could step out on the mounting blocks on either side.

Harry waited to assist Buck and Keene with their parties as Chillie led the first visitors up the rounded steps onto the small front porch. The candle lamp in the lunette above the door was lit unnecessarily, but was an extra welcoming touch.

They entered to see a large marble table crowded with wedding gifts. The children stood at attention on the staircase. To the right of the front door, the large bowl of Winesap apples was in its usual place. On the opposite side was a black horsehair sofa with needlepoint pillows under a set of Napoleon prints. Across the room, a Confederate hat hung on a point of an elk's antler.

The photographer tried to set up a camera but was pushed to and fro by people rushing in to get out of the chill. They paused only seconds to scan the wedding gifts before pirouetting to take in the foyer with its gray-washed walls spacing Virginia walnut doors rounded to fit seamlessly into the circular room.

"Don't worry," Nanaire told the photographer. "They will move into the dining room soon enough. And I'll see that a few hang back to give you a good picture."

"Thank you, ma'am."

Irene served as guide to "grandpa's" wing of bedroom, bathroom and sitting room, built to balance the dining room on the other side. Nancy took the ladies up the stairs to see the four bedrooms and bath. The children had disappeared.

Nora ushered guests into the dining room where Auntie Ann and Fannie presided efficiently over the buffet. At first the guests were shy about eating another large meal. However, Chillie encouraged them heartily, suggesting first the beefsteak in thick gravy.

"Come on now," he said. "Try those snap beans and yellow squash and the stewed tomatoes with peppers and okra. Auntie Ann has been working on those all morning. Don't forget the cookie cutter biscuits. Yum!"

As the photographer's subjects filed in to fill their plates, they spread the word about gifts from the Vanderbilts and Astors, packed by people from Tiffanys. Solid silver candelabra and leather cabinela, two rich dressing cases, and scores of other articles which must not be missed before departure.

As manservants helped guests back into the wagons, Chillie turned to give Nanaire a satisfied kiss goodbye. "I better see them back to the hotel and make sure they all get on their way home.

Memories Will Always Linger

I hope Mr. and Mrs. Brooks are still there so I can say a proper goodbye."

"You go along now, Chillie. I will see you over there later."

"You don't have to. . . ."

"Yes, I do," his wife declared. "Nancy and Nora are coming with me. John is taking us over in the carriage. Nancy and Phyllis lost a locket, and we have to go find it. You know, it's the one that rider brought up at the last minute a few days ago. We don't even know who it's from."

"Right," Chillie agreed with the plan. "When I get to the hotel, I'll ask Edwin about a place to stay in Waynesborough tonight. I imagine his staff will want to spend the time cleaning the Brandon rooms."

"Great, sweetie." She squeezed his hand. "Emily already has packed the bags. Robert, Irene, Dana and the boys are staying here.

"And, Chillie. It was wonderful. Wonderful beyond words."

* * *

"I don't know where it could be, Nanaire," Nancy said in exasperation. "I mean, the room was a mess. You saw it. But, Irene and I went through everything when we came up to change after the reception."

"Maybe the maids picked it up in the towels," suggested Nanaire. "Or, wasn't the window open? Maybe. . . ."

"I had Harry check around outside," said Nancy. "Nothing."

"Well, it's not in here," Nanaire agreed.

"Let's organize a treasure hunt," suggested Nora. "There are still many guests here and. . . ."

"Go find your father . . . please!" Nanaire said impatiently.

Nancy made another sweep of the room, checking against the door frame and even under some feathers, as they waited.

"Chillie, we cannot find the locket," Nanaire said as he came through the door. "Why don't you have Mr. Goode offer a reward for it?"

"A splendid idea, Nanaire. What did it look like? It would have something inside, right?"

"It was a silver heart on a chain, oh about sixteen inches long," Nanaire said.

"And, it had some kind of swirl engraved on the front, I think," said Nancy.

"Did you or Phyllis open it?" Nanaire asked.

"No. I was just taking it out of the trunk drawer when it got caught," said Nancy. "When I pulled, it just flew off."

"And, no one knows where it came from?" asked Chillie.

"Not yet," said Nancy. "Someone may mention it at a party later. But that will be so embarrassing."

"We have been embarrassed before," said Chillie, the twinkle in his eye belying his somber tone. "I don't think anything can beat Irene wearing the palm leaf on her head that Easter. She was determined to have a hat even if we had not two bits to our name."

"As I recall," said Nanaire, "you threatened to wear confederate bills in the shape of a handkerchief in your frayed coat pocket that year, my dear."

The 1893 nationwide financial depression truncated Basic City's potential, Adelia learned in her research. And, the monetary panic of 1907 sealed its fate as just another small Virginia town.

Reese's steel furnace was never built in Virginia. The inventor returned to Pittsburgh where he continued amassing a total of one-hundred seventy-five metallurgical and steel processing-related patents. He also discovered that the phosphorous-laden slag produced in the rival Bessemer process made great fertilizer.

The Langhorne wedding was the last great event at the Hotel Brandon which became seasonal lodging. However, its amenities and reputation continued to attract guests from across the East.

What of the locket? What had the Langhorne's done to find it? Had the mysterious jewelry lost its romantic interest in the sisters' high society whirl. Phyllis's marriage ended in divorce, as did Nancy's. The older sister made the best second catch.

Adelia wondered, "Who sent the locket? And, what was in it?"

Chapter 7

"Look what I found, Mrs. Robinson," said Mary as the hotel manager stepped into the office. "I was cleaning behind the desk and found this old notice." She held up a message hastily penned on the back of a laundry shirt card.

"Do you remember a big wedding several years ago? It says here that the bride lost a locket and her daddy offered a big reward for it. I wonder if they ever found it."

"I don't know, Mary," the manager replied. "The search was popular community entertainment for awhile. But things have changed so much in the last seven years."

"Geoffrey just found some lumber scraps from construction during the wedding," Mary said. "Saw a dinner program sticking out from a pile in the carpentry shop.

"He was complaining so loud," she mocked. "Pricked his poor wrist on a nail as he reached down to get his hammer. Screaming about someone just throwing things under the work-bench."

"Well it hurt," Geoffrey said, walking through the door and reaching out to grab Mary's wrist to tap it smartly.

"They were making changes in the rooms and were not quite finished when the Langhornes moved in," allowed the hotel manager. "I suppose the locket might have been gathered up in some scraps in the room or out in the hall."

"My sister said townfolks heard about the reward and were looking all around outside—in the planters and rhododendrun. Said there were boards and scrap materials hidden up behind those bushes."

"Let's go look, Geoffrey," Mary said, pulling him toward the office door.

"Might as well get Charlotte and David to help," the manager said. "Then you'll have time to finish cleaning before those five families arrive tomorrow for the long weekend.

* * *

"We've been looking for hours for that stupid locket," complained Geoffrey.

"More like an hour and a half," said Mary with customary precision.

"Anyway, it's not here," the other girl said. "I guess she didn't care too much after that big wedding and a honeymoon to South Carolina and living in New York and all."

"How do you know all that, Charlotte?" Mary asked.

"Oh, my Aunt Margaret talks about the Langhorne family all the time," she explained. "The bride . . . Her name was Phyllis. Her sister, Nancy, married Waldorf Astor a couple of years ago. . . ."

"The one who built that big hotel in New York City?" David asked.

"No, that was his father," said Charlotte. "But Waldorf was rich, too. They moved to England, to Cliveden, a great house on the Thames River." Charlotte adopted her aunt's sophisticated tone. "She says Nancy always wears a sprig of lemon-scented verbena pinned to her brooch. And she goes around giving out dark caramels from America."

"Well, I want to find the locket," said Mary. "It would be great to wear to Harriett's big party tonight. Talk about going in style. Daryl's picking me up in his father's REO."

"At least you get to go to the party," said David. "I have to stay and run the telephone and telegraph."

"Oh, please," said Geoffrey. "None of us will be going if we don't get back upstairs and finish clearing the porch and sweeping the rooms."

* * *

"Good morning, Mrs. Robinson, is it?"

"Yes, sir. Welcome to the Hotel Brandon."

"Thank you. I am Mr. Harris from Roanoke."

"Yes, sir. We have you in room two twenty-eight, down on the north end by the turret. That is the room . . . Oh well, never mind."

"Not the room of the ghost, I hope."

"Oh, no. We don't have ghosts." Her tone was more a titter than the reassurance intended. "There was a wedding here several years ago, and that was the bride's room. She lost a locket. The staff had a kind of treasure hunt yesterday. Not in the room, but in the carpentry shop to look at scraps from the construction. Oh, dear. I go on and on."

She reassumed a managerial posture. "It's a beautiful room. Here is a pamphlet about the hotel and grounds. What brings you to the Hotel Brandon, Mr. Harris?"

"It's a nice half-way point to Charlottesville and convenient for the trains. My son, Timothy, is thinking of matriculating at the University of Virginia. We plan to go over and get a feel for it."

"Excellent. Do you have the train schedule?" she asked helpfully. "We could put together a picnic lunch for you to eat on The Lawn. That's the long yard between the original buildings, down from the Rotunda. Walking the lawn and picnicking there are traditions."

"That sounds very nice, thank you," he said. "Oh, here come Timothy and his mother now. I will tell them about the picnic and the locket mystery."

"Harry will take your bags up."

* * *

"Good Morning, Mr. Davis isn't it?"

"Yes, ma'am. How did you know? Have we met before?

"I don't think so," the manager said. "I noticed the White Sulphur Springs tag on your bag, and I was expecting guests from West Virginia."

"Excellent deduction," he said. "We want to try some different spring waters. According to your brochure you have hot lithia baths."

"Yes, sir, and cold ones, too," she responded, giving the usual spiel. "Soothing for gout, rheumatism, kyspepsia, general debility

Memories Will Always Linger

and kidney trouble. But, oh dear. I hope you and your family are not ill."

"Not at all," he said. "We just want to enjoy the weekend."

"I thought we might go to the Brunswick Inn this afternoon," said Mrs. Davis, stepping to the registration desk. "A friend attended a weekend landscaping class there several years ago and went on at length about the gardens."

"Be sure to tell Miss Renfrow that you are staying here. I'm sure my assistant will see that you are well taken care of," Mrs. Robinson said.

"Oh you own. . . ."

"I manage the Brunswick now," Mrs. Robinson explained. "Mr. Loth died in nineteen-aught-four. We are pleased to offer two outstanding hotels for our guests. The Brunswick just reopened for day guests yesterday."

She shook her head. "Mr. Pierson, who owned the hotel until recently, replaced the boiler with a still so we can't have overnight guests for another two weeks or so."

"You have heat here?!" said Mrs. Davis quickly and breathlessly.

"Oh yes, the latest in steam radiators. And your room has a fireplace," the manager replied gently. "Press the electronic bell to the right of the door should you need any assistance here or in getting to Waynesboro.

"Mr. Davis you may want to try the clay pigeon shoot at the Brunswick while your wife enjoys the gardens. The children. . . ."

"They are really young ladies now, and I am sure they will enjoy some hiking," said their mother. "Or, I understand there is a room for bridge and mahjong."

"Yes there is," the manager affirmed. "Very good. You can take the trolley down to the Brunswick and back. Or we can arrange a canopied carriage at either end. You will be in room two fourteen here. Geoffrey will take your bags."

* * *

"Good morning," said Mrs. Robinson. "Welcome to the Hotel Brandon."

"Good morning. I am Mr. Guise. From Virginia Beach. I'm afraid we're in a bit of a hurry. Trying to catch the train to Natural Bridge."

"Certainly. Here, fill out this card, and I'll have Geoffrey see to your bags."

"May I ask why you chose the Brandon, Mr. Guise. I mean, we love to have you. But there is, I must say, a grand hotel at the bridge."

"My wife insisted. Her mother was here at the anniversary ball in 1891. I'm sure Mrs. Guise will enjoy looking around tomorrow," he said doubtfully after scanning the lobby.

"Okay then. Your room—two twenty four—will be ready when you get back," the manager said.

"David, take Mr. Guise down to the station in the runabout. Your family is still there, are they not."

"Oh, yes. Little Henry was quite taken by the boy with the wooden tray around his neck, hawking Chesterfields, matches and sweets," the guest replied. "And Mrs. Guise is securing fried egg sandwiches at the station diner."

"I am sure," said Mrs. Robinson, trying not to show her disdain. "Have a fine day. Perhaps you will join us for our sing-a-long this evening in the parlor."

"Come along sir," said David, donning his goggles and cap "Step up a bit now, sir. Those balloon tires make it rather high."

"Ah-ooh-gah," the horn sounded as they sped down the gravel path.

* * *

"Good afternoon. Welcome to the Hotel Brandon. My goodness, what a cute little girl. And boy," the manager added, as the mother caught him at the foot of the stairs.

"Good day. I'm Mr. Sangle. From Richmond. We are here to explore the Luray Caverns."

"Oh, dear. I'm afraid you have missed the train for the day, Mr. Sangle."

"We will go tomorrow. Today we will rest."

"Good idea, sir," Mrs. Robinson said looking at the boy poised to run toward the other side of the lobby. "We'll have dinner beginning at seven o'clock, in the ballroom, just down that hall. Southern baked chicken, potatoes, snap beans. Perhaps some spaghetti for the young ones. And strawberry shortcake for all."

"That will be excellent," said Mrs. Sangle, a bit breathlessly.

"You will be in room two hundred, just at the top of the stairs." Away from the other weekenders and far enough away from the season's guests at the other end of the hall, the manager mused. "David will bring your bags up in a few minutes." And a key to lock the doors to the porte-cochere balcony, she remembered.

*　*　*

"Good day, Ma'am."

"Good afternoon, sir, and Mrs . . . it must be Longrin."

"Yes, indeed. From New York," he replied.

"Welcome to the Hotel Brandon. You have come a long way," Mrs. Robinson grinned a little at that. Her guests did not seem to notice.

"I hope it will be worth it," said Mrs. Longrin. "My aunt was here for the Langhorne wedding. She was a bridesmaid."

"Well, isn't that interesting. We were just talk. . . ."

"Hey, come on," Little Michael Guise said, grabbing the arm of the Longrin child, who was almost swallowed up by the steamer trunks. "They have a tetherball here."

Lawrence looked at his mother, who nodded.

"We will see that he gets to your room, Mrs. Longrin. You are just down the hall from Michael—I believe it is—and Mr. and Mrs. Guise, in room two sixteen. Harry will take your trunks up, and you can relax awhile before dinner."

"That will be so nice," Mrs. Longrin said. "Mr. Longrin has a headache. Do you. . .?"

"We have a drugstore right here, with a soda fountain," the manager said, smiling. "You may want to treat the young boys tomorrow."

"Yes, a good idea," Mrs. Longrin agreed. "We all needed to get away from the city. It's so exciting with the zeppelin, and the new tunnel, and the Ziegfeld follies. However, I especially wanted Lawrence to get some fresh air and have a little fun. He is turning into a little Einstein and doesn't have many friends at the club."

"Indeed," Mrs. Robinson replied formally, but liked the thoughtful wife and mother. "I'll have Harry bring up some headache powders with the trunks, and Mary can run a hot lithia bath. Be sure the windows are opened up all the way. The fresh air will be good for all of you. There is no trouble with mosquitoes here."

* * *

"It'll be another beautiful sunset, David," Mrs. Robinson said as they stood on the arcaded porch after she checked to see that dinner was going well. "Gorgeous enough to paralyze, as we say in our brochure."

"There will be a nearly full moon tonight, too, Mrs. R."

"Yes," she said. "I think we'll start the sing-a-long tonight with that new tune, 'Shine on Harvest Moon'. We'll have a good harvest of cash from our guests this weekend," she laughed.

"Maybe Timothy Harris will play the violin," offered David. "Geoffrey said he had a handsome alligator-hide instrument case."

Operations at the Hotel Brandon turned a major corner in 1913, moving from entertainment and tourism to education, Adelia learned as her research continued. Her life was changing, too. Her part-time job at Kinko's supplemented an inadequate income from consulting. She loved her public relations work and the successes on each project. However, sufficient clients were elusive. And she grew increasingly diverted by the mystery of the locket.

Friends visiting from Michigan gave her opportunities to show off Fairfax Hall and a few favorite places across Virginia. Their late afternoon arrival left only minutes for Adelia to say, "Make yourselves at home" and suggest what they might find to do in Waynesboro before she rushed off to work. Late that night, she got back to find them both, and Mollie, contentedly watching TV.

"Oh, we've had a great time," Andrew said. "I shot some video of the outside to show everybody. It's really interesting.

"When we went into town, I went off the wrong way where the main street splits, and I just bounced back over the curb at the hamburger place." Lyn rolled her eyes.

"And, Mollie and I had a nice nap. . . ."

"What!" Adelia exclaimed. "I spent all day keeping her off that bed so you wouldn't. . . ."

"It's okay," Andrew said. "She just came right up. It was fine."

The bed, of course, is Mollie's territory, her half in the middle.

A few days later, as they prepared to drive off, Adelia remembered a recent surprise in the sleeping quarters. "Did you happen to wake up and see anything, well, strange in the bedroom?" she asked.

"As a matter of fact, I did," Lyn said. "Some little green lights near the ceiling."

"Um, yes. Forgot to tell you about the fireflies."

Adelia supposed the Hotel Brandon guests sometimes saw the creatures on warm nights. Then she wondered how frightened—or inquisitive—the young Brandon Institute students were upon their discovery.

Chapter 8

"Quite a ceremony to dedicate the new library this morning," the business manager said to the Brandon Institute's top administrator as they relaxed in the president's office.

"Yes, it was a good event for the older students, Howard," he replied, considering a short stack of books on his desk. "Perhaps they learned more about the value of books and what a difference young persons can make in their community."

"You may be right, Elmer. I hadn't heard that story about the beginnings of the Waynesboro library before," Howard said. "Imagine how proud the members of Mrs. Steven's Sunday school class at the First Baptist Church must be right now." He shook his head in wonder. "It has come a long way from the small library they ran on Wednesdays and Saturdays for three years."

"The class held a book shower to bring in donations to get started," Elmer said. "I don't think they mentioned that today. Then, when they learned about the state loan program, they had to talk the men's Sunday School class out of their larger room. And with the Massachusetts acquisition, they finally moved into the Wayne Inn."

"Did you ever meet Virginia Leftwich, Elmer? The mayor said she was a member of the class and served as the first librarian off and on for over a year." Howard related. "She resigned last summer to go to China as a missionary."

"That's interesting," Elmer replied nonchalantly. "Maybe we can use that state library program until we get more books in our permanent collection, Howard. It'll save us some money to get fifty books at a time on loan." He penned a note on his desk blotter.

"And, let's encourage Miss Moon to help her students apply today's lesson," he continued. "Maybe her commerce class can come up with an idea to raise money."

Elmer adjusted the shade of his desk lamp which hung a little crookedly on the tall, curved brass pole. "Celia Howardson is in that class. You know, our student from California? She was very impressed with the fund raiser to buy the book collection from the New England library.

"Imagine," Elmer said, twirling a pencil. "Everyone turned out for the party on the Fishburne drill field. The Basic band played, the bakery gave away ice cream, and women from all over the city made cakes and candy. The electric company even supplied the lighting set up free."

"No wonder it drew the Carnegie Foundation's attention," said Howard appreciatively. "We were first in the state to receive the incentive grant to become a Carnegie Free Library. One of three in the whole commonwealth."

They discussed how several of Waynesboro's most prominent citizens were library proponents, including the Pratt, Loth and Rife families. Howard noted the group's foresight in purchasing a lot near the top of Eleventh Street and holding it for the right time.

"James Fishburne was in that group, too," said Elmer. "He has that house just down the hill, next to the military school. It was the first residence in Waynesboro with running water and bath."

Howard abided Elmer's enjoyment of the detail, then initiated a more somber discussion. "We better get started on any fund raisers for the institute right away. I fear this war is going to mean a lot of changes."

"Do you really think the assassination of an archduke in Austria will get the United States involved in all those European struggles?"

"I certainly hope not, Elmer," said Howard, but recited the warning signs. "The bankers talk about costs going up. Reilly says the railroads are receiving notices from the government about shipping emergencies. And Grady, at the Penn Foundry, says they may be producing military armament at the Car Works plant.

"If Wilson does get us into this fight, American men will be going to war," he added. "Some of our older young men may be called to serve here at home."

"Always the watchful business manager, Howard," the president said appreciatively. "Do you remember when Wilson came through on his way to Staunton to celebrate his election? Had an old-fashioned homecoming at the Presbyterian manse, I hear."

"I, of course, was not in this area then," he continued. "But I heard about it from Harvey. He's sure proud about joining the Basic Fire Company Band and getting to play the tuba at the station that day."

"Harvey is always proud of something," Howard chuckled knowingly. "But I know that Mr. Hildebrand is happy he comes each week to give French horn lessons."

"I hope these new upgrades are not going to put us in a bind," Elmer said, looking through a sheaf of papers on his desk and handing some to Howard. "We're getting substantial notoriety—of the good sort—about the institute. Look at these letters from all around on the east coast."

"There's one here from Texas and one from Washington, even New Mexico," Howard said, nodding.

"We just invested a lot of money on those Packard pianos," Elmer said, doing calculations on the blotter.

"Now who is sounding like a business manager, Elmer? We'll be all right," Howard said brightly. "People appreciate your emphasis on academics and business training. But, more so, opportunities for their children to get a good grounding in music and art. I still expect our enrollment to top two hundred next year."

Elmer looked up as a grin spread from a memory. "At least these renovations are not so extensive as the ones two years ago. I walked in that June to see an army of men putting up and removing partitions, cleaning up the second floor, and installing mountains of blackboards, desks, and other paraphernalia.

"I heard a lot of hard words, I tell you, about sealing the glass doors of the ballroom which opened out on the porch," he continued.

"Imagine, though, controlling all those students at each meal without closing them in."

"As I recall, there was another concern about controlling students. The very idea of mixing boys and girls in a boarding school," Howard said in mock horror.

"I still have parents—and ladies of the town—who do not think the partition between the second floor wings sufficient," laughed Elmer.

"Surely the credentials of Elmer U. Hoenshel, D.D., educator, traveler, writer and lecturer, have overcome that," intoned Howard.

"Our success may be attributed more fully to our vice president and director of music, E.T. Hildebrand of the Hildebrand-Burnett Music Publishing Company of Basic. And to a very strong faculty," Elmer continued the verbal applause.

"It's true we're considered one of the best music schools in the south. But, the most important criteria for the mothers is always well-furnished student rooms and sanitary toilets and baths. We have Mrs. Morris to thank for those," Howard made a slight bow from the waist even sitting in his Windsor style chair.

"I suppose we should praise Mr. Tenner for the beautiful grounds, however much the young women on the northeast end complain about the noisy birds singing in the coppice outside their windows. Of course, access is no longer so easy to our vine-covered arcaded porch," Elmer said with comic contempt. "The new green lounge chairs do make the walk through the foyer and across the entry porch worth the effort, though."

"Let us not forget the easy accessibility of the school to all. Sixteen passenger trains a day stopping at Basic and only a three square, five-minute walk from Union Depot to our hallowed walls," bragged Howard. He appreciated the rail service that brought students from D.C., New York, Philadelphia, Baltimore, and even Cincinnati, St. Louis, and Chicago.

"Our reasonable rates must make it worthwhile. So much learning and culture for two-hundred, three-hundred twenty-five dollars for a whole session." Elmer tipped an imaginary hat to his business manager.

"Oh, it's good to talk about our success so cheerfully, Howard. We are too often mired in the details," said Elmer. "I suppose we should make more effort to reward our hard-working students with some gaiety. Why there are two motion picture theaters in Waynesboro now, and the skating rink and bowling alleys. Even a gun club." He paused.

"Say, do you think we could take them up to see Swannanoa?"

"I don't know, Elmer. The new macadamized road across Afton Mountain certainly makes transportation easier," Howard allowed. "I'm not sure, though, that Major Dooley, Esquire, will want to open his fifty-two room villa to our gang. Even on their best behavior."

"Check it out, Howard. It could be a very educational experience," Elmer urged. "Our students can see the, er, financial virtue of hard work and get some history lessons at the same time." The president made another note on his blotter.

"I've not been there myself," he continued. "However, I understand the decor includes oak and walnut paneling, three kinds of marble, frescoes, and a teakwood, mosaic-adorned fireplace. I'm still trying to picture that."

"My wife, Deborah, managed to acquire an invitation to an event there," Howard tried to say without bragging. "I must say I don't care for that mantelpiece of randomly embedded pieces of wood, much less for the matching screen above it." He shook his head at a memory of the Near Eastern look so oddly fashioned.

"However, I do so adore the marble double-staircase with the one-hundred-thousand-dollar Tiffany stained glass window on the landing," Howard said with mock haughtiness. "You know it depicts a Grecian scene with a romanticized version of Dooley's wife. She named the place in honor of an Indian tribe once native to the area, by the by."

"Speaking of culture, Howard. I want to take the older girls to the production of 'Pygmalion' next month at Miss Baldwin's Seminary in Staunton. Some of them may want to continue their education there."

Elmer extolled the virtues of a curriculum offering further language studies, more science, extensive studies in moral and natural philosophy, and opportunities to continue their music and art.

"And what of the young men, Elmer? I suppose we should take them to Charlottesville to see the university."

"Did you know," Howard interjected, "that Swannanoa includes the site of the Leake Tavern. That's where Thomas Jefferson and the Rockfish Gap Committee met to choose Charlottesville as the site for Central College."

"Soon to become Jefferson's Academical Village." Elmer smiled at the name.

"I suspect, though, that the boys would be happier checking out the new garage down at the Waynesboro Automobile Company," said Howard. "Or joining the game just down from Maple Hill."

"What game is that?" Elmer asked.

"I had lunch with Mr. Bowman recently at the Basic City Café," Howard began to explain. "He showed me an essay by his son, Clifford. It was quite good. Seems boys often use the cow lot at Sixteenth and Main as a baseball field 'despite the stumps', it read, 'and even though the cows do not appreciate the finer points of the game.'"

"Oh, my. What a picture I just had of that," laughed Elmer. "I can't imagine chasing a ball in left field while having to watch out for cow patties!"

Howard leaned forward toward the desk to look Elmer in the eye and say, "You made the right choice to establish your institute here, Elmer. The facilities are good. The resources are excellent. You have Elra Oaks, a most comely chalet house right down the street. One of the best designs available from Sears & Roebuck, if you ask me. And you have two nice towns of people to support you and add a little diversion now and again."

"I can do without the diversion in the saloons on Commerce," Elmer pretended to grumble. "I hear an argument broke out again Tuesday night and Henry had to restore order."

"You mean by unbuckling his peg leg and whirling it over his head by the belt," Howard described the method with a chuckle. "That man is a character. You would think the reappointment of the Belmont Hotel would help the situation down there."

Elmer sighed and leaned back in his chair, saying, "Do you ever wonder if the world is passing us by here, Howard?"

"You mean like the suffragette march in Washington D.C. last year. Or being the first to see D. W. Griffith's *The Birth of a Nation* or hear Carl Sandburg read his *Chicago* poems. Or hear the first news about the opening of the Panama Canal?" Howard listed a few headlines.

"No I don't miss it that much. I can always take the train to New York City like the Duponters," he said, reflecting on a recent experience. "White coated service in the diner, smooth ride, catch a few winks in the Pullman. Take in a little ragtime in the city and enjoy the ride back. Costs about twenty-five dollars for the train. And, I'm sharing the rails with a carload or two of our finest Rose Cliff Orchard apples."

"Sounds good," Elmer admitted, "as long as they don't have a three-locomotive smash up as they did last year near Dupont."

"That was quite an accident, Elmer, but no one was killed," Howard allowed. "I just pray we never have another disaster like the one in the Rockfish Gap tunnel in 1910. They never were sure what happened exactly."

"What do you mean?" asked Elmer.

"The C&O Number Three was coming through, and one car was occupied by Italians on their way west, most of them asleep," Howard said. "Apparently one of them woke up and saw smoke in the car. You know how it seeps in as the train goes through that mile-long tunnel, even with Crozet's ingenious system of capturing the smoke in inverted tubs and washing it out with water." Howard looked away from Elmer's lowering lids, realizing the danger of getting carried away with a favorite subject.

"Anyway, the man must have cried fire and people panicked," Howard continued. They couldn't get out the back of the car so they started opening windows, which let in more smoke."

He quickly related the story of Virginia Roncali, an eighteen-year-old girl who fell off the train, her family's search for her along the tracks, and the tragedy of finding her in the tunnel, cut in two.

"They carried her out, and the Number Thirteen brought them down into the station," Howard finished and added, "Several townspeople took the Roncalis in for awhile and saw that the girl got a nice burial."

"What a tragedy," Elmer said solemnly. "You know, Guy Hamilton and I had lunch recently, and we talked about some of the customs around here.

"He said that if someone dies out in one of the rural areas, a friend of the family goes to the church and taps the bell for the number of years of the deceased's life. That's better than the big city any day," he concluded.

The knock at the door brought them both to attention.

"Yes, Bessie," Elmer said. "Come on in."

"I just need to file some of these papers before I go home," she said.

"Oh, I didn't realize it was so late," said Howard, rising a little in his chair to pull out his pocket watch. "By the by, Elmer, have any of the construction people found a locket?"

"What locket?" Elmer's head lifted from scanning under his desk for his other shoe.

"You remember, Bessie, don't you?" Howard asked. "A few months ago you found that old sign caught in back of the desk drawer. It offered a big reward for a locket lost at a wedding. Who was it?"

"The Langhornes, I think," she replied, not much interested.

"You mean the Civil War railroad tycoon?" asked Elmer.

"That would be his work after the War Between the States, Elmer," said Howard with customary southern correctness. "Yes. One of the daughters, Phyllis, was married here and her lost locket has been a mystery ever since. I imagine the family has long since forgotten it."

Howard told Elmer about the oldest daughter, Lizzie, who died in Richmond the previous year followed shortly by her husband, Moncure.

"They were quite young, in their fifties I believe," he said. "They lived most of their lives in the shadow of war and reconstruction. Folks say she always wore black and had her hair pinned up in big rolls on either side of her head." He shook his head sadly at the war's aftermath.

"The rest of the siblings went to Europe," Howard continued, "except for one son, Buck. I believe he's still at the Mirador estate. You pass it on the way to Charlottesville, Elmer."

"The new Emmanuel Church across the road was dedicated to the memory of their mother, Nanaire, last year," contributed Bessie.

"Another brother, Harry, died of tuberculosis a number of years ago," Howard said, ending the family summary. "I wonder what the rest of them will be doing in Europe with war breaking out."

"I guess that could be a problem," sighed Bessie. "I can't even imagine being that rich.

"We lived on a small mountain tract near Sherando," she explained. "Daddy had a saw mill, and we all got up at four in the morning so the boys could get the horses ready to go to the mill and take the lumber into Waynesboro. I had to carry in the wood and water and help cook. Mama sewed for the family, even all the bedding." She took out a handful of papers to straighten a file.

"In the summer, Daddy sheared our few head of sheep, and Mama washed and dried the wool. Then I had to pick out all the loose dirt and burrs so that it could be carded," she continued. "I picked so much I could hardly see, getting soooo sleepy. Sometimes there was so much dirt, I would just throw some wool away. It was too bad if Mama caught me." She conscientiously straightened another group of papers.

"I always looked forward to Christmas dinner at Grandma's house. Deep snow on the ground and the big fireplace going full blast because the front door was hardly shut with all the going in and out to play in the snow." Her eyes brightened at the memory. "At twelve o'clock we all sat down to eat. What a feast—ham, potatoes, beans, bread, desserts, and lots of milk to drink. Her voice trailed off.

"Oh, I'm so sorry," she said, embarrassed. "I've been standing here jabbering."

"It's all right, Bessie. Howard and I have been doing the same most of the afternoon," Elmer said. "Your memories add to the general consensus that this is a good place to live, even if we must put up with some discomfort or delay now and again."

As Howard and Bessie left the room, Elmer turned around to the walnut secretary behind his desk to look at papers for the next day's meeting. The committee would consider a merger between Basic City and Waynesboro.

They were returning from a walk to the back of the property that crisp, early spring day. Adelia knew the groundhog had emerged from hibernation because Mollie's run, off-leash, was even more frantic and full of zigzags and loops than usual.

Working at her computer last fall, she glanced out the window and saw a strange creature in the yard between the perpendicular wings. It was very fat and much too low to the ground for a feral cat. As it entered some covert hole in the foundation under John's wing, Adelia pulled out the encyclopedia CD and started searching. She wondered if it was a woodchuck and found it was either that or a groundhog. They were the same animal, defined by its habitat. Fairfax Hall had open land and woods.

Daly called from the back entrance, holding Bo back from exploding through the portal.

"There's an old man in the entrance hall. He says he's been talking to you about a missing locket here."

"Okay." He finally came back in the daytime, she thought. "Thanks, Daly. Tell him I'll be right there after I put Mollie upstairs."

"I can take her up. He seems to want to see you right now."

"Thanks, Daly. I appreciate it. Can you hold on to Mollie's leash real tight, Bo?"

"Hello," she called, rounding the corner at the foot of the stairs.

The old man was staring into the triptych mirror over the fireplace.

"I'm sorry. I don't even know your name. Mine's Adelia."

"Well hello, Adelia," he said with a faint pant of relief. "I'm Gerald. Made it during the day this time."

"You sure did," she encouraged. "Let's look around a bit."

Adelia was surprised by his lack of interest in the ballroom and porch. His gaze lingered then rose as they came back to the stairs. Daly was crossing from the hallway near the office.

"Daly, I'd like you to meet Gerald," Adelia said. "He came by a couple of times, but always at bedtime. I said I would show him around if he got here during the day."

"Yes, and I finally did," Gerald said with a touch of bravado. "Adelia and I have been discussing my memory of a locket being lost here."

Daly glanced at Adelia, eyebrows slightly raised. "Never heard of it."

"I think it was lost during a wedding of one of the Langhorne sisters at the turn of the century. . .," Adelia started to explain.

"Can we go up to the cupola?" the old man asked just above a whisper.

"I don't know, Gerald. It's a pretty good climb up these stairs, then staircases to the third floor and attic, and then two up to the top."

"I can help if you really want to do it," Daly chimed in.

"What about Bo? It's going to take awhile," said Adelia, hoping to discourage the trip.

"If it's okay with you, Adelia, I'll take him up to your place and give him strict orders to sit on the day couch with Mollie and watch TV—and not move."

"Sounds good, if you're up to it, Gerald," said Adelia, mustering enthusiasm.

"Let's go," he replied brightly.

The regular staircases were not a problem; the three took them slowly. As they reached the stairs to the first cupola level, Adelia stopped Gerald with a commanding touch and said, "Are you sure you want to do this?"

"I've got to." He was breathing hard but Adelia could not tell whether from exertion or excitement.

Daly climbed up a few steps and reached back to give him a hand up as Adelia steadied him from below.

"Be really careful, Daly. Gerald. The floor up there is a mess."

"It certainly is," Daly said, and Adelia knew from her tone that she had not been there before.

"Oh, this is grand," Gerald said, walking around slowly, leaning liberally on the railing, but with a very satisfied smile. Then he slowly sank to the floor.

"I'll go get some help," Daly said and was not gone two minutes before returning with John.

"Well, well. What . . . Are you okay, Mister. . .?"

"I'm fine, son. And it's Gerald."

"Looks like you've had a little too much excitement for the afternoon, Gerald," John said, looking around disapprovingly at Adelia and Daly.

"Now don't go getting on them," Gerald said, struggling upright. "They were very conscientious and thoughtful. I just had a spell. I'm all right now, if you'll help me down."

Daly went to get Gerald water while the old man and Adelia sat and John stood in the entry parlor.

"I could light a fire," John said. "It's kind of nippy now."

"That's okay, young man," he said as he accepted the water with a "Thanks" and nod to Daly.

"I better be going. No—now, everyone, I'm all right. It was a wonderful adventure. I hope I didn't scare you too much." And he was up and heading quickly for the door.

"I'll see you soon, Adelia, to talk about our little mystery."

Chapter 9

"Well, I never. I cannot believe they did it. What will their parents think, John, if they hear about it?" His wife did not wait for a reply.

"Imagine bobbing their hair so short just because you told them they could not. It's just, well, peckerheaded."

"Let's hope the parents don't find out, Frances," he said. "It's a good thing this happened after May Court. And, that they need my permission to send telegrams or use the phones."

The head of Fairfax Hall School for Girls and his wife were relaxing in his office. An hour before, the dean called them to review the students lined up in rows on the stairway. Upon receiving a pillowcase of multicolored locks, from a petite redhead whose hair was particularly short, the president named the punishment and sent them back to class.

"We'll have many very bored young ladies after being campused here for two weeks of spring. It'll be worse than the chicken pox quarantine in February. On the other hand, we should have some good bridge and mahjong tournaments," his wife said straightening an inkwell.

"Maybe we can have a fashion show," she suggested brightly. "The girls can be mannequins, like models showing the latest fashions at society affairs—with complexions of milky white and deep carmine lipcolor. They could wear hostess pajamas. Anna has one of those cute blouses with the puffed sleeves and sailor collar."

"Really, Frances!" her husband almost yelled in exasperation. "I hope they devote the time to their end-of-term papers."

"Miss Crawford gave her students a creative writing assignment on that locket," replied Frances.

"What locket?" John asked, even more perturbed at the unknown.

"You've not heard?" Frances replied. "Apparently it was lost at a wedding when this was a hotel. A large reward was offered, but it was never found."

She paused to think where the story started. "Mrs. Ferguson heard about it from her friend who helped search for it as a young maid for the Hotel Brandon."

"Intriguing!" John said more for his wife's sake than from real interest.

"Even more so," she said. "One of the sisters in the wedding, Nancy Langhorne, married Waldorf Astor and became the first woman in the House of Commons when he died. Some might say she is in sympathy with our students on this one," Frances mused aloud. "She's known for unusual behavior, especially against old-fashioned tradition."

"Great. I shall leave that item out of our history lessons," John declared, reaching for his reading glasses and typed sheets of notes. "Tomorrow I continue talking about the important things like President Wilson's train pulling into stations across the nation to sell the League of Nations. Wilson was so hoarse he could hardly speak, but I will never forget what he said:

> I bring a message of gravest impor-
> tance that is indeed for the entire world.
> Winning the war is not enough; now we
> must also win the peace.

"We turned him down, Frances. He had that horrible stroke. And, I fear our senators' rejection of the world peace organization was a grave mistake." He lay the notes down flat on his desk.

"American interests are different now, John Noble Maxwell. Women have changed since they worked during the war," Frances said, her tone reproving. "Why, many of the ladies in Basic and Waynesboro were proud to become farmerettes. Those that were not already," she added. "Women have had the right to vote for almost two years."

"And we have flagpole sitting, dance marathons, those jug-jug-spit motorcycles"—he sounded the words—"and caterwauling horns on automobiles," John said with exasperation. "Is that progress? That is not what we are trying to do here."

"Of course, dear," Frances soothed, smoothing her skirt along the seat of her chair. "I think over one hundred students from thirty states and Santo Domingo confirm that we made the right move. Coming from West Virginia to establish Fairfax Hall—well, this whole region needed a fine finishing school for young ladies." She strove for encouragement, citing a fine faculty—especially the two from Wellesley and Vassar.

"I'm just so happy that we waited until after the Spanish flu and the infantile paralysis scare," she continued. "Can you imagine the whole town—two towns—quarantined?"

"Tell the young ladies about that one." John said, obviously fond of the idea. "It'll make them feel better when they crab about not going to town for their Coca-Colas and hot chocolate sundaes with pecan nuts and whipped cream."

"I don't think those fads will fly very far in these new days of calorie counting," Frances said firmly. "However, we could give them an occasional treat like hot dogs and lemonade or chicken a la king or peach cobbler."

"Dr. Richardson might approve an occasional culinary indulgence," John allowed, making a note on his desk calendar. "Mr. Rubush will see they get plenty of exercise in the riding ring. Miss Best can lead extra calisthenics on the porch," he added enthusiastically.

"Dean Bradford—She has really made a fast transition from Mt. Holyoke," Frances included an affirmative judgment. "Miss Bradford suggests we encourage instructors to hold as many classroom sessions outside as possible. Perhaps it will help the young ladies release some pent-up energy." She stood to stretch and look out the window at the late-blooming redbud trees on the lawn.

"I think most of the faculty will go along with that," John agreed quickly. "I'm sure Miss Bell will welcome new art subjects. Maybe they can find new floral patterns for their china painting. It's more difficult to imagine Miss Raymond rolling pianos onto the back lawn," he chuckled. "Flute and violin lessons perhaps."

"Moving home economics and domestic science may be hard, and certainly typing will be impossible." Frances considered the logistics. "But I can make the adjustment in shorthand. And language studies can take on a whole new meaning."

"Tres bon," he agreed.

"John, I think it can be a good end-of-year change, especially for the ladies ready to escape with their one-year cultural diplomas," Frances said, thinking about going to the kitchen for some tea. "And it will help the second-years prepare for the more independent schedules of college."

"Perhaps one or two of the ministers would like to take advantage of the open night sky for their devotionals," John said, joining his wife at the window. "Maybe Dr. Walthall, newly from the Presbyterian seminary, or Rev. Edwards. He is quite progressive for a Baptist, don't you think. Chaplain John should approve of expanding the universe of meditation."

Frances rolled her eyes, but touched his shoulder lightly. "All the better to help our students develop faith in eternal values of life. The parents like that," she emphasized, "while schools like Bryn Mawr are very happy that our graduates have a non-sectarian grounding in academic subjects."

There was a sudden loud crash from above, followed in a couple of minutes by an appearance at the office door by a workman in paint-splattered overalls with hammer in hand.

"Sorry, Mr. Maxwell, sir. I wanted to tell you straight away that everything is all right," he spoke quickly. "We were moving some boards for the windows on the third floor, just over there—he pointed upward toward the end of the hall—and the barrow tipped over. No harm done. Didn't hurt the floor or anything. Hope it didn't startle you too much."

"That's okay, Hank. The ladies should be in their classrooms," John said. "However, please ask Mrs. Williams next door to check the closest rooms on the second floor."

"Yes, sir, Mr. Maxwell. I'll do that right away. And, I'll tell the crew to be more careful. Mind their p's and q's," he said, backing out with a tip of his cap.

"Moving classes outside will get everybody away from all this noise of constructing the new third floor," he sighed, leaning against the window sill as his wife returned to her chair. "And, when are they going to finish renovating our house, Frances? I don't know how much more of this I can stand."

"Just a little more wallpaper in. . .," Frances broke off when she saw the look. "It's an old house, John. Built at the same time as the hotel. I still don't know how we shall deal with that unbearably narrow bathroom."

"Frances!"

"I know, John," she said, changing the subject quickly. "The dormers are going to look nice here, and we need space for dorm rooms on the third floor. Hard to believe it was once just space for the er necessary tasks.

"Frances." He said the name with a cautionary tone.

"At least they've not found any skeletons up there like they did at the Mountain Top Tavern on Afton," she teased.

"Lilly, down at the dress shop, says there were always rumors of ghosts there," she continued, leaning forward into the story. "And when they tore out some walls last year, there were the bones. Her husband says they are from some wealthy drovers who stopped there around the turn of the century. Never heard from again."

"Ghosts are all I need with this construction and the merger," said John. I'm already haunted by the good folks from Waynesboro, and especially our own Basic City, over bringing the two towns together."

"That's the joy of being mayor," she teased.

"Just look at these proposed names," John said, going behind his desk to pull a sheaf of papers from the top drawer. "Basboro, Waynona, Waynola, Wayne City, Waynapolis. Spark Plug, for gosh sakes. That one must be from Frank Harper down at the Ford dealership in Waynesboro."

Elizabeth Tidwell

"At least you got the new sanctuary built at the Methodist Church," she said for encouragement. "The stained glass windows are going to be so pretty, and the pews are so much more comfortable."

"Oh, yes. Just fine and dandy," he said mockingly. "We are still getting complaints from the men who miss the old weatherboard building where they sat down by the stove at the front where the spittoons were."

"You need a break, John. We all do," Frances said. "After this campusing is over, let's take the students down to the Star Theater for a Saturday western. Of course, they'll have to put up with the town boys cheering for their favorite cowboys and snickering when the heroes put their hats over the horses' eyes as they kiss the girls."

"Or we could take them down to Ed Palmer's new lithia beach at the stone dam," she offered. "It's just upstream from the Basic-Waynesboro bridge. That will be an appropriate place to celebrate the pending merger, don't you think?"

Adelia wandered once more through the arcade with its wrought iron light fixtures that fit the stuccoed building's Spanish ambiance, which was muted somewhat—she mused—by the faux half-timber on the sides. She passed the gymnasium's entrances, checking each door again to see if it was locked. The windows were too high for Adelia to see inside, except to the sunlight streaming in the fenestration high on the east wall. The handle on the door closest to the main building turned.

Pushing the door inward, Adelia faced a staircase down and one up from the small landing. There was no entrance to the ground floor gym. She descended to an indoor pool, about two-thirds junior Olympic-size and very dry from years of disuse. Tiles along the edges gave the depths.

As she circled the swimming area, she glanced out low Palladian windows at the thicket growing toward the main building and at another overgrown space to the east. Previous exploration revealed seven levels of open-iron-grates set in wooden frames for steps on the east side. They led down to a locked door at the bottom of the structure. Mollie hated the steps and usually threaded her way through bushes and vines beneath and on the sides.

Up an eight-foot slope of dangerously crumbled steps was the east wall of a wide pit about ten feet deep. A toppled pine engulfed the barrier. At one time, John told her, trucks backed up to the pit and coal spilled down to feed the boiler on its west side. Later a natural-gas-fired boiler was placed in the basement along with a swimming pool filter fully four feet in diameter.

Climbing the inside stairs to the third level, Adelia discovered four small rooms. These must be the music practice rooms mentioned in the yearbooks. A former student told her workmen found marijuana seeds in the pump organ when it was moved.

Since she saw the two-story orange brick building from three of the rooms' windows, Adelia knew they were the ones high on the stucco facade. She did not find access to the two balconies on the south end of the gym nor the lower ones on the east and west sides pictured in a yearbook.

Outside again, she traversed the covered walkway to the main building. Dark wooden timbers above looked old but sturdy. The slate path beneath just as sturdy but not as aged. The shingles on top were red to match the ones of the gym, not the green ones of the main building.

She tried the door into the north perpendicular, surprised to find it unlocked. She climbed a few steps and walked past pegs where coats and hats of the Montessori students hung during the winter. She tried the door into the auditorium; it did not budge. Disappointed Adelia walked through to the main hall and up the back stairs to the second floor. She must arrange a time with Beverly to see the school's main rooms.

Mollie and Adelia sometimes caught Beverly and the students outside at recess or working on a project. Last week, they were planting flowers in beds along the windows that looked down into the basement rooms.

"Wipe your hands like this," Beverly said loudly, demonstrating by brushing hers briskly together, as the students charged the white dog. Mollie shied away a little before giving into enthusiastic petting from relatively clean little hands.

No enthusiastic little ones today. On Saturday, school was closed.

Chapter 10

"Evelyn Byrd is so excited." The dean practically burst into President and Mrs. Maxwell's parlor in the headmaster's house. "She was spending the break in New York City. They got the word Saturday that her uncle, Richard Byrd. . . . She shares his middle name, you know," she interjected and paused to catch her breath. "He flew over the South Pole the day after Thanksgiving. That makes him the first to do both. He did the north pole in twenty-six."

"That certainly is cause for celebration," said Frances, offering the coatless Carrie Vaughan hot cocoa sprinkled with cinnamon. "I'm surprised she didn't stay in New York for the big party."

"Oh, the South Pole expedition is continuing. Evelyn will return for the homecoming when her uncle sails back in April," Carrie explained. "Perhaps she'll see the Goodyear blimp, Pilgrim, cruise over if it is there for a salute."

"You know, Frances, one of the reasons Evelyn came here was the new facilities," said John.

"Yes, indeed," she replied enthusiastically. "Adding the pool down the slope has made that area so much nicer. And I really love the new drive and terrace out front—even at the cost of ten thousand dollars."

"Commander Byrd was more impressed, I think, with the gymnasium and indoor pool," her husband said in a dignified tone. "He is very serious about physical training. Maybe we can convince him to make a donation in commemoration of his achievement to help pay off that sixty-thousand dollar debt." He emphasized the "that."

"A possibility, John. At least, maybe, he could lend us his famous name," Carrie offered cautiously. "I believe, though, that the family first heard about Fairfax because of that freight car crash in 1922, before the gym was built."

"It was in the Richmond paper and even one in the capital," Frances affirmed, relaxing more against the needlepoint pillows at her back. "I'm sure it made the New York press. News travels fast when it involves the railroads, especially when both the C&O and the N&W are involved."

"It's a miracle that only one person was killed," said John. "Later in the afternoon, some students might have been in the N&W station ready to leave for a weekend trip home."

"I can't even imagine the sound—oh, the horror—of watching that freight car go through the siding block at Delphine and then careen across Commerce," exclaimed Frances, leaning toward Carrie. "Doly Vines was lucky to get out of the way as it came through the roof."

"You're right, Frances. I overheard two girls talking as I went down the hall after lights out," the dean said. "They had sneaked downtown for sundaes at the drug store. I should have given them red notices. But it was punishment enough that they couldn't tell everyone about the experience."

"I have a feeling they told the story many times out on the trail rides and hikes," John replied with a chuckle, setting his cup on the end table and shifting it onto a doily as he caught his wife's eye.

"Speaking of hikes, John. Evelyn and Dottie will receive their letter in that activity at the athletic banquet," Carrie said. "They did it the hard way, tackling the last fifteen miles on a trip with Mr. Smith up to the gates of Swannanoa and back."

"There are easier ways to get in one hundred miles in the fall," the president said, raising his left eyebrow.

"Isn't Dottie the one with the full length black and white coat that she, shall we say, must take care not to wear in the rain?" asked Frances, grinning and shifting forward on the couch.

"Yes." Carrie grinned back. "I don't think skunk pelt coats will be a major fashion hit. I've not seen them in the news reels."

"Carrie, did we get a copy of the reel of Coolidge visiting here last year," John asked. "I want to show it to my history class before the holidays."

"Afraid it slipped my mind. There's a copy of the newspaper in the library," the dean offered apologetically. "The picture shows our young ladies greeting the president at Union Station on Thanksgiving Eve and handing a basket of flowers to his wife."

"Our students, the Fishburne cadets, the Boy Scouts, and the Waynesboro Municipal Band. I bet Coolidge was just happy to get into that bullet proof Lincoln and start the drive up to Swannanoa." John laughed so hard his elbow shook the end table. "He almost left Mrs. Coolidge and that chow dog behind in all the hustle and bustle."

"Another good deed for the girls and good press for the school. Speaking of, I received letters from nine of the needy families the girls helped with food and clothing this Thanksgiving," Carrie said.

"Mr. Beardsworth asked me yesterday about playing Santa for the Christmas party, and he is going to get Jerry Smith to help him find a big tree," she continued. "Those poor little children have such a good time taking the stockings down from the mantle and getting the presents from Santa."

She turned again toward Frances. "Your niece is in charge of gathering the candies, nuts and fruits this year," she warned. "You better guard your pantry."

"Jerry has that big farm over at Staunton," John said. "I bet they have some nice trees. We're fortunate he travels here to take care of the horses."

He got up to take a book from a shelf behind Carrie's chair. "Now Jerry is a living history lesson. Meet the man who shoed General Black Jack Pershing's horse in the Argonne Woods of World War I." He opened the volume to a picture of the farrier hammering in a nail next to a tent and handed it to Frances.

"Oh, John. You are incorrigible," said his wife, passing the book to Carrie. "Are you going to read 'The Night Before Christmas' in front of the roaring fire? Or shall we have the dramatic club act it out?"

"Both. A wonderful idea, Frances," he replied, retaking his seat.

"It's a shame Evelyn will miss the Fairfax Player's skit about the Langhorne locket this spring," Carrie said, placing the book on the floor next to her chair. "It has become quite a tradition. They'll get to use the new stage curtain for the gym. And Evelyn earned the part of Nancy this year."

"She could have enjoyed her own notoriety in a historical way," mused John.

"This must have been some hotel at the time of the wedding," Frances said. "That reminds me. The Brunswick renovations are really nice. They completed them just in time for the workers at that new Dupont plant to move in. They're going to make something called acetate. The two hotels were very competitive early in the century."

John ignored the jumble of sentences.

"Speaking of the Langhornes—I hear the youngest son, Buck, is still living the pleasurable life of an eighteenth century gent at a farm near the James River," he said. "It may be near where the tornado came through in May. Lost a lot of apple trees in those storms."

"I hear Buck can cut the rug when he ventures out," said Carrie.

"I don't know how long anyone will be stalking the cat's pajamas," John tried to pick up the lingo and failed. "We've not yet felt the worst of the crash on Wall Street. I'm worried about how it will affect us. I expect we will have to do some careful budgeting."

"We'll not have to cut back any programs, will we, John?"

"Well, we may have to raise the wood working fee to sixty dollars, Frances," he teased. "No. This year we'll keep core academics the same. We do need to decide what programs will attract the most students for the next few years."

He mentally considered a few possibilities from his planning sheet. "We can utilize some public school resources for the general academic program and concentrate our attentions on the college prep side. We'll certainly have to look at continuing the junior college."

"We also have to consider this year's spring events, John. Change the spring outing from Mount Vernon to Monticello." Carrie said. "And, we better ask parents about expenses involved with May Court."

"Let's look on the bright side, Mr. History," Frances teased. "We celebrated the golden jubilee of light a week before the crash. Moving the new radio across the street to the entrance foyer wasn't easy. But it let all the girls hear that wonderful program."

She looked fondly at the big console model across the room. "You could almost see President Hoover and Thomas Edison reenacting that first successful light bulb test from the restored laboratory in Michigan.

"It'll be hard to beat that at your radio parties for awhile longer, Carrie," Frances continued. "However, I'm sure your guests have retained their enthusiasm for *Dixie's Circus and Novelty Band.*"

"If not for the *Stock Market Report,*" groaned John.

"Have you heard Evelyn's news?" Sally shouted the question as she raced through to the kitchen.

"Yes, we have. And what are you doing young lady?" asked Frances. "Where's your coat?"

"I'm getting some of those pretty paper napkins we found in Washington this summer. We're having a party."

"It's too late. And I was saving those for. . . ."

"We might as well go and join the fun, Frances. Carrie," John said, getting up to retrieve coats from the hall closet. "Tomorrow we start some serious planning."

Adelia stopped the car at the end of the Afton Inn parking lot. Her timing was perfect. The sun would set over the mountain spur in a few minutes.

She spent the day with Mollie on the Blue Ridge Parkway, enjoying several scenic turnouts for views of both the Shenandoah Valley and Nelson County to the east. She could not recall the name of the valley on that side.

However she loved to drive down there, taking old Route 250 on the south side below Interstate 64. Someone told her a Greenwood tunnel terminus was near the parkway crossing. She would have to look for it someday and then take her favorite local road—the near perpendicular Route 6—down to Route 150. The first time through the winding rural roads she came across the monument.

"That was the name," Adelia thought. "The Tye River Valley." The monument honored people who died in floods caused by Hurricane Camille.

Occasionally she continued down the road to a very curvy section in Amherst County past Crabtree Falls, taking the back road to Lynchburg. She planned someday to hike back to the falls. Today Adelia and Mollie tested their endurance on Humpback Rock along the Appalachian Trail. She must get in better shape.

She thought of her friend, Tom, who finished his first Appalachian through hike—from Georgia to Maine—just before his fortieth birthday. He called Adelia on his second trip through, and they had supper after a quick look at Fairfax Hall.

Her nephew and his wife enjoyed hiking in Shenandoah National Park on the north side of the Afton Mountain divide that spring. They loved Central Virginia, experiencing it while Scott worked a Richmond construction project for his Dallas-based firm. "I hope she'll choose either Texas A&M or the University of Virginia," Scott told Adelia as she held his baby daughter the next Christmas. She understood completely.

Clipping on the leash, she took Mollie for another short walk. As she looked out toward Waynesboro, not quite into the setting sun, Adelia wondered how long she could afford to stay in the area.

Chapter 11

"William Benjamin Gates, you're getting water all over the new carpet. Why didn't you leave your coat and galoshes on the porch outside the office?" His wife, Fanny, was seated in a chair close to the entrance hall fireplace, thinking seriously about having it lit, even in late April.

"Every inch of space is taken out there," he said, hooking his slicker on a hall tree and putting the galoshes on the hearth. "Dean Scranton won't let the girls leave their things in the halls. Says it will make the flooring peel. She's probably right about that.

"There are more riding clothes drying in the stable's leather rooms than tack he continued, thinking about lighting the fire. "And coats are spread out on the hay in the loft. But, Harry Nash, down at the *News-Virginian*, says it is almost over."

"What's the total?" his wife asked.

"Just under ten and a half inches in two days," he replied, adding, "Elwood said some of last night's third shift workers at Dupont had to walk the elevated railroad and across the C&O bridge. Took the N&W to the plant.

"I found Elwood polishing silver early this morning," Bill continued. "He can't get home, so he's staying up at the Sunset ranch, in the stables with his cousin."

"I talked to Mrs. Patterson this morning on the telephone." Fanny continued the dire weather results. "Mary says the dogwood blossoms are gone, even up on the Blue Ridge. And a lot of the redbud. Her brother-in-law, Alfred, called her with a botanical damage report from the ranger station in the George Washington Forest. He knows how she loves the foliage." She paused before the good news.

"She says the azaleas will 'flame beautifully,' even with this downpour," she said, joining her husband on the couch, observing a discreet distance "She is so proud of Alfred. He helped organize some of the Civilian Conservation Corps boys for forest patrols, you recall. Then they were recognized by President Roosevelt when he came through to dedicate Shenandoah National Park last summer."

"That was an experience. That is, the president's trip through town," said Bill. "Stopped at Union Station and waved at everyone from the back of the Ferdinand Magellan. That's what he calls his special rail car. Did you know that the train is called POTUS? What do you think that stands for, Fanny."

"President of the United States, of course," she replied with mock haughtiness. "Charlotte mentioned it at the dinner table that night. She was more excited about seeing Eleanor. She's from upstate New York, too, you know. Most of the girls were gushing over Fala, that cute little Scottish Terrier. They miss their pets."

"After this has dried out, we can take them out to the farm to see the pointers," said Bill. "Give them a lesson in milking cows, too. They will have a new appreciation for the dairy co-op."

"Oh, yes, they'll love that," she said, stretching out the word "love" and hitting him lightly on the shoulder. "I'm sure they'd prefer attending the *News-Virginian* cooking school if they have it again this year. They'd get much more useful information about food values and the cost of living.

"However," she said, indulgently, "I suppose you want to don your canvas hunting pants and coat and show off your farm."

"We better get over there before the Blue Ridge Parkway crews destroy all the roads into the area," he said in affirmation. "Tom Gitchins supervised down at the North Carolina line during the first stretch. Said the roads into the mountains are totally inadequate for the heavy loads, materials, and equipment." Bill paused to ponder the potential damage to his land.

"He seemed to be happy with the workers, though," he continued. "Tom said Coxey's Army is inexperienced but intelligent and willing to labor."

Bill added that most were earning thirty cents an hour, but some received a dollar and a half. "Either way, it's grueling work from the clearing and grubbing to the asphalt paving," he said, shaking his head and getting up to light the fire.

"I'm just glad the Virginia General Assembly finally ceded the land. All that fighting over taxes and civil legal matters," Fanny said, motioning for Bill to move his galoshes. "After all, the planning started right up on Afton when they were looking to extend Skyline Drive to the Smoky Mountains. The engineers stayed at the Brunswick Inn."

She noted that work on the Jarman's Gap to Rockfish Gap segment finally started only four months before, although the survey was completed in September of thirty-three. "Our very own eight-and-a-half miles of the two-hundred twenty-five miles in Virginia," she said proudly.

"Never can tell about public facilities around here," Bill said, retaking his seat. "Dr. Hubbard moved the Waynesboro General Hospital site from Jefferson Park to West Main because of lack of sewerage. Now he's afraid it won't open on time."

"It better," Fanny exclaimed. "Dr. Weems and Dr. Watkins have made it clear their Wayne Avenue facility will close at the end of August." She wondered how many would be affected by a gap in facilities.

"How far we have come from Dr. Weems's maternity home in 1934 to three floors of first-rate facilities in the summer of 1937," she continued. "Do you think the hospital crews are using any of the materials from the Brunswick Inn?"

"I wouldn't be surprised," Bill said. "It's hard to believe Mr. Dorrier reopened it in thirty-three then tore it down three years later, selling the lumber and fixtures for scrap." Bill shook his head.

"I guess the workers at Dupont's acetate expansion had their own houses by then, he mused. "But the town youngsters can no longer skate on the porch. And I failed to get the lights for our lobby and dining room."

He leaned his head over the back of the couch to admire the globes with the gold accents. "But, I like these better."

"Bill, how long do you think it will take to clean up from this storm?" Fanny asked, preferring to watch the fire.

"Not very long, I think. Compared to last year's Great Spring Flood"—he emphasized the three words in an uplifted tone—"this one is mostly an inconvenience. Those three additional inches of rain last March flooded at least two more stores up the slope on either side of Main Street. Dupont had to close."

"I will never forget that trip over here, said Fanny, turning slightly toward her husband. "The ground was so soft—two weeks later! I didn't know if that old Model T truck was going to make it the hundred miles from Henry County; the touring car didn't have a chance. But we did need to talk to Mrs. Maxwell and her sister again before the final decision to buy the school," she said emphatically.

"It was April 2," she continued. "I remember because, before we could leave, you had to issue demerits to some of Blackstone College's young gents for that April Fool's stunt."

"Yes. It's good to have my own school with fine young ladies learning the social graces. Though nothing could be graceful in this muck," he said wearily.

"I was looking through the yearbooks yesterday afternoon. They had a beautiful walnut secretary and spinning wheel in the parlor," she said, glancing over her left shoulder at the now sparsely furnished area and back to her husband with a curt look.

He stared resolutely at the fire.

"There are many traditions at this school," Fanny continued, ticking off a list. "The freshman party with everybody dressed as babies, spooky Halloweens, Christmas parties for the needy, the annual basketball tournament among the classes, the YWCA initiation, the senior May breakfast, cultural trips to Charlottesville and Staunton, May Day skits. And, of course, one of your favorites, the Valentine Dance with the Fishburne Military School cadets."

"Well, the young ladies also have dances with cadets at the Staunton Military and Augusta Military academies." Bill stressed the last word with a slight mock, proud that he was on the Fishburne Military—school—board. "I am partial to Fishburne. And, don't forget the excellent training in academics and sports at Fairfax."

"Yes, dear," Fanny said. "I've seen the stacks of new postcards ready to be mailed, thanks to members of the new Scribblers Club taking time out from their prose and poetry. Here's one," she said, taking the opportunity to stretch her legs as she retrieved a card from the office.

> A nationally-known preparatory school and junior college for girls, located at Waynesboro, gateway to Skyline Drive and Blue Ridge. Graduates successfully transfer to all leading four-year colleges and universities. The departments of Music, Art, Dramatics, Secretarial Science and Physical Education offer excellent advantages to those interested in a terminal diploma course. Enrollment is limited to 180 for boarding. Alumnae in 44 states and 19 foreign countries.

"Well, we are the Miss Porter's of the South," Bill said. "However, not that many in Virginia would be impressed by a Connecticut school."

"They'd be impressed if we were better known," Fanny said, pausing at a new idea. "Maybe we could get two or three girls on *Major Bowes Amateur Hour* touring show. It may come back to the Paramount Theater in Charlottesville next year.

"The girls were so disappointed this year that the singer they call 'Blue Eyes'—Frank Sinatra, he is—was not on the tour. But they did love the organ program before the show." She ran out of breath, but not ideas.

"Say, maybe we could persuade Constance Bennett to use us as a site for one of her movies. The girls would love it."

"I don't really think we want that kind of notoriety," Bill replied quickly. "*Affairs of Celini, Moulin Rouge, Outcast Lady, Ladies in Love*? Really Fanny!"

His wife pressed on. "You know, Bill, she is supposed to come by again Sunday to visit her niece. The girls will be marcelling their hair and trying on new styles all weekend. Snug pink sweaters and white skirts, spiked heels, French step-ins."

"Fanny! They better stick with the white middy blouses with blue sailor collars and pleated gray skirts. Well, not those two things together, of course," he laughed and threatened: "If things get too out-of-hand, I will revoke senior privileges, and they'll not be able to take the horse trolley into town. The service is celebrating its first anniversary of revival next week, come to think of it."

Fanny rolled her eyes at her husband's ubiquitous use of historical trivia and picked up the teasing again. "Some of them are beginning to wear her cosmetics. They usually sit around after church and luncheon, waiting for Miss Bennett's car to drive up. However, it could be different this time."

"Why is that?" he asked politely, only mildly interested.

"A different kind of excitement," she said. "Laura and Cassie. Laura is the freshman from Ohio who is so good with the stage sets for the Fairfax Player productions. Mary Cline sparked her interest in art, but Laura chose the larger canvas."

Bill rolled his eyes at the side track as she continued, "I hope Mary will stay in school for her senior year. She is so smitten with that artist, Arthur Dintenfass from Philadelphia. I am afraid she will follow him up there."

Her grimace at the thought brought out her cute dimples, Bill thought.

"Anyway, Cassie—her name always reminds me of Chessie, the new C&O cat mascot. Cassie is the junior from Ottawa who was so devastated when King Edward abdicated the throne last December to marry Mrs. Wallis Simpson."

"But, this weekend, Laura and Cassie are doing what?" Bill prompted.

"Organizing a treasure hunt Saturday afternoon," she replied and began to explain. "Laura heard about the Langhorne locket that was lost here at the turn of the century when the original hotel was rented for Phyllis's wedding.

"Laura is convinced that it was gathered up in all the towels in the bride's room and slipped into a niche or corner of the laundry," she continued. "Many things have changed in this building over the years. But the laundry has always been in the same area."

"Well, make sure they get brushes and trowels and what have you. Maybe we'll have the cleanest laundry ever," Bill brightened. "Probably the cleanest place in the whole campus with this weather."

"If she comes up with that locket, the ladies will have to reorganize the May Day celebration. The show would rival the colonial ball and skit in celebration of the bicentenary of George Washington's birthday four years ago." Fanny got caught up in the possible excitement.

Those graduates would be so envious, she thought, reading about the locket's discovery in the *Faxette* alumnae paper. She reached to grasp her husband's hand discreetly against the couch cushion just as he leaned forward to stoke the fire.

Driving past the church and to the foot of the pasture, Adelia saw an older woman tending irises in front of the school's old main entrance. Like other Fairfax Hall gates and surrounding fence, it was made of irregularly sized granite stones, heavily but attractively mortared. The slope and fifteen-foot conifers screened the building along most of this end. However, there was a clear view from the gate and about twelve feet on either side, once you walked right up to the enclosure.

"Hi, I'm Adelia. I live up at Fairfax Hall," she said in greeting after parking her car on the side street.

"Well, good to meet you, Adelia. I'm Katherine," she said with delight, putting down her large green-plastic watering can to shake hands. "I heard there were people living up there now. That's good."

"Your flowers are very pretty," Adelia echoed the contagious lilt.

"I try to keep them up," she said. "We own the pasture; bought it at the big auction. We really wanted the land over there." Katherine swept her arm to the north. "You see what happened to it," she said with disgust, looking at the rows of closely spaced small houses where the school's playing fields once clustered, unseparated from the main grounds by the current road.

"We had to bid on this property to keep that from happening here," she continued. "A lady up at Dooms asked us to keep her horse while she was away, and she hasn't come to take it back. That's PJ." She indicated a steed of indiscriminate color walking slowly from one tuft of grass to another.

"Do you live around here?" Adelia asked.

"Right over there in the brick house," Katherine said, pointing. "Pat has lived there since 1934 and around here all his life. I lived in Crimora until we got married; forty years ago it was.

"I don't know how much longer we'll be able to keep this land up. But we won't sell it if there's a chance it'll go to a developer," she said firmly.

"It would be a shame to lose the view," Adelia agreed. "It's awesome from Fairfax. And it's nice here, too."

"Do you see the little path there?" Katherine asked, pointing slightly to the right. "Marked with the granite stones—just above the edge of the ground?"

"Sure. I've noticed the stones up at the flagpole terrace," Adelia affirmed.

"See how it separates, rounding out on each side to form the open space?" Katherine continued. "The girls used to come down the path *every Sunday morning to attend church there."* Katherine pointed to the columned portico of the Basic United Methodist Church across the street. *"And they were so pretty in their white dresses for graduation."*

"Speaking of graduation, do you know where the Laurel Chain ceremony was held?" Adelia asked. *"Some yearbook pictures from the fifties show the girls encircling two pines, about six feet high or so."*

Adelia paused to picture them. "I can't find them, even allowing for substantial growth. The trunks must have been about ten to twelve feet apart. The middle area between the paths would be perfect."

"I don't remember two pines together like that," Katherine said quickly. *"We must have pulled thirty truck loads of dead trees and limbs and brush out of this pasture after we bought it. Hadn't been picked up for years."* She seemed to grow tired just talking about it.

"I'll ask Pat; maybe he knows," she said. *"Why don't you come over some day and visit? Just knock on the front door. Don't trip over the kitty's box."*

"Thanks, Katherine," Adelia acknowledged. *"I'll look forward to seeing you again and meeting Pat."*

As she drove her Toyota past the semi-circular drive entrance, to the back lot, Adelia thought she saw the trunk of a large black car as it headed down the hill on the other side of the porte-cochere. She hurried through the back hall of the building and into the foyer. There was no one there to tell her if she missed an old man's visit.

Chapter 12

"Oh! That was a loud one. What a night! We have a good view from here on the terrace." Carolyn was standing in front of Fairfax Hall with another teacher, watching Waynesboro celebrate the end of World War II.

"Swann Marks took a few girls to the cupola for a better view of the fireworks and porch lights," said Margaret. "They probably can hear more of the horns honking, too. They're not buffered by the trees."

"It's fortunate not too many girls are here yet for the fall session. Too many up there would bring the roof down," said Carolyn, with a chuckle. "At least, with the war over, the rest should be able to get here more easily on the trains."

"VJ night, August 14, 1945," mused Margaret aloud. "I am so thankful we got the message to tune in the radio to Truman's speech. He sounded great—but sort of sad. About the bombs dropped on Hiroshima and Nagasaki, you know. They sound awful." The English teacher knew she did not yet grasp the full import of those two events.

"Do you think you can work a little of the science into a special Vespers talk tomorrow, Carolyn? It's a good opportunity to show the relevance of science. And everyone needs time to reflect on its consequences."

"I will try," the chemistry instructor said doubtfully. "Not much of the science is known outside the government. But some information has leaked out since the first bomb was dropped last week." She remembered the rumors for several years that the Germans were building an atomic weapon and that the United States "liberated" a few of their scientists to build one of her own.

"I guess tomorrow will be like the Tuesday after Germany surrendered," Margaret said, reviewing the expected sequence. There would be no special announcement at lunch or celebration assembly with just a few students. Essential government operations would remain open downtown. But many of the retail stores, professional offices, and restaurants would close with a blast of the city's fire siren.

"I don't think we'll get another special edition of the *News-Virginian*, Margaret said about her favorite part of the celebration. "They saved newsprint from their 1944 quotas for the three sections after VE Day. I doubt they have extra left."

She seemed lost in reverie for a minute. "The stories were so strange because most of it was preprinted before Roosevelt's death."

"That's the radio broadcast I'll never forget, not that I actually heard it," Carolyn said. "Remember, Elsie came running in from the kitchen during supper to whisper in Mrs. Gate's ear. Her son heard the news on the radio during the *Juvenile Adventures* broadcast. He called her to say President Roosevelt was dead and to ask what a cerebral hemorrhage was."

"The junior college students and faculty got together the next morning to hear President Truman on the radio and join in a period of silent prayer for the GIs still fighting," Margaret said, sitting down on the terrace wall. "We finished by singing 'America.' It started kind of soft and ended very proudly. Then we had a regular schedule of classes," she said quietly, grateful when the other teacher sat down close beside her.

"You missed all that, didn't you, Carolyn," Margaret asked rhetorically. "You and Norvelle went to Charlottesville that morning to see the funeral train go through."

"Yes," she answered reflectively. "That was the quietest I've ever seen a train station, even at six-twenty in the morning. The special train just moved through slowly. No noise except the wheels and the whistle—and so many people weeping. Only took twenty-three hours from Warm Springs to D.C."

"Sure was different from 1941 when FDR came through on the way to Staunton to dedicate the Woodrow Wilson birthplace," said Margaret. "A 'new shrine of freedom,' he called it."

"There was a big welcome banner over the N&W railway underpass and the Waynesboro Municipal Band playing," she recounted. "Eight to ten thousand people there on a Sunday morning, according to the newspaper. The reporter said people traveled here by car, truck, and on horseback. Then the Secret Service sped him off to Staunton, flanking his car with that motorcycle escort."

"It's a real shame he didn't live to see the end of the war," mused Carolyn aloud. "Hmmm. Like Wilson, he didn't get to see the United States lead a world peace organization. At least we joined last month when the United Nations was chartered."

"I'll never forget the memorial service the Saturday after FDR's death, or the four days in-between," said Margaret softly, looking down at her swinging feet. "Four days of reminiscing and nothing but somber music on the radio. And then the service down at the Basic church."

"Held at the same time as the funeral in the East Room of the White House," Carolyn contributed.

"Swann started the organ prelude at three-thirty," Margaret recalled. "It was a good service. Pastor Courney and Pastor Truitt, from down at the Presbyterian church, did a nice job with the prayer and scripture reading. But Swann's music set the tone."

Her sudden chuckle surprised Carolyn. "That was one time we didn't have to worry about girls hiding in closets so they wouldn't have to go to church," Margaret said.

"I was afraid all the fun of the spring session would be lost," said Carolyn. "Miss McClure said she was having a hard time getting girls to work on the May Day celebration. But VE Day saved that."

"We have all sacrificed so much during the war," sighed Margaret.

"Use it up, wear it out," Carolyn started the chant, and Margaret chimed in with "Make it do, or do with out."

"I am so glad it's over," Margaret continued. "I'll be so happy to have butter, steak, sugar—and nylons—again." She mentioned some of the industries that changed to war manufacturing. No new cars since forty-two when Detroit converted to tank production. And Dupont switching from rayon to acetate for the soldiers' uniforms and gear.

"The C&O—maybe it was the government—spent quite a lot of money to rebore the tunnel through Afton Mountain last year," added Carolyn.

"You don't suppose Richmond or Washington thought they would need to transport goods through there like they planned for the Civil War?!" said Margaret as though the terrible possibility had just occurred to her.

"No. I don't think anyone expected the war to come over here," Carolyn laughed a little at that. "But, there were German U-boats along the East Coast."

"I'm sure the girls will be ready to resume the traditions of dear old Fairfax this year," said Margaret, more brightly. "What a great spirit they had during the war, though. Helping with the clothing drive for Europe and donating blood for the Red Cross."

"And helping the Fishburne cadets and German prisoners of war harvest the local crops at Sherando," added Carolyn. She remembered aloud how several girls saw Dr. Watkins for blisters and bruises. "You remember the doctor," she prompted Margaret. "He started the first hospital here and is now the physician for the POW camp."

"I don't know him. But I did notice the enthusiasm of the girls," Margaret said. "They must have contributed five hundred pounds of clothing for those poor people in Europe. A five-and-a-half-ton total from Waynesboro." She shook her head in wonderment. "I bet Martha Hyer put in thirty pounds herself before leaving for Northwestern University in Illinois."

"By the by, I received a letter from her last week," Carolyn said. "She got a reading with Paramount Studios. But she hasn't heard anything back yet."

"One hundred percent participation in the blood drive was impressive, too," said Margaret, remembering the Fairfax spirit.

"Not to mention the rolling of hundreds of miles of surgical bandages at the Lutheran church kitchen."

"Yea!" Carolyn and Margaret looked back toward the Fairfax Hall roof at the loud cheer and saw two long blue streamers unrolling in front of the cupola.

"Why, I believe Miss Marks has given up some of her prize streamers from University of Virginia basketball," Margaret said. "This really is a celebration!"

"It was really too bad about Toni Redfern," Carolyn continued the wartime reflections. "She was a swimmer here in the late thirties and had a good chance to make the 1940 Olympic team." Her disappointment for the graduate was obvious.

"And poor Kathy, Elizabeth, and Renée," she continued. "Their fathers were, probably still are, in dangerous situations. The diplomatic corps has to deal with so many things at their posts without knowing a lot about the war negotiations."

Margaret stood up to stretch. "I think a couple of the girls will miss sneaking out to Peck's Barbecue for dancing and to meet the young men in uniform," she said with a wink, although Carolyn missed the emphasis in the dark. "I can't believe they didn't get caught!"

"That is really amazing," Carolyn agreed, grabbing the hand offered to help her up. "Betty got caught just going down to the Southern Restaurant to get some eggs one day. 'Needed to get some protein,' she said."

Margaret began walking along the terrace. "Remember the big controversy in 1939 over the military mind set promoted by the cannon near the high school football field?" she said. "The cannon was eventually melted down to supply metal for the war. But I do believe Commandant Hudgins mentioned the travesty to General George C. Marshall when he attended the final spring review at Fishburne in 1940."

"Don't forget the big luncheon at the General Wayne Hotel when Greer Garson came to sell war bonds," said Carolyn. "Some of the girls helped serve lunch.

"Fried chicken, corn pudding, lima beans, and peach ice cream are a pretty good reward for buying a hundred dollar bond," Carolyn said, licking her lips a bit and remembering how little supper had been eaten this evening in all the excitement. "All those women—they called themselves the Waynesboro Women's Army—went house to house to canvas for those bonds."

Margaret was enjoying the conversation but decided to get some exercise by walking down the lawn. Her recitation of memories changed direction, too. "The students really enjoy the new dorm wing. Not so new really since it opened in 1939. And we got the Sunset Ranch. The girls are delighted with the extra riding space, one-hundred and thirty-five wonderful acres back to the Blue Ridge."

Carolyn followed down the hill, asking if Margaret remembered the excitement over Pocahontas, the horse with the perfect-shaped Indian head on the side of its neck and top right foreleg. "The picture was in *Ripley's Believe It or Not*. I believe the girls meant to take up a collection to buy it. But even Henry Ford would not pay the asking price of twenty-five thousand," she chuckled.

"Then Janet Burks discovered the Plumb place," Margaret remembered aloud. "She heard about it while eating lunch at the drug store one Saturday. The soda jerk told her that 'Happy' found an 1835 flint lock pistol and a ten-inch Civil War knife while adding a floor to the smokehouse."

Margaret related how the fountain attendant convinced Janet to go look at Happy's Indian arrowheads and the artifacts he traded for from all over the United States. "He has over twelve thousand items in a two-room building he calls The Shack," she said as they reached the front gate.

"I don't think President Gates is too keen on it, but several of the girls go over there regularly to see the artifacts and hear Happy's yarns," Carolyn added, leading back up the hill. "Can't be too bad. The local schools and the Boy Scouts take field trips there."

"Isn't Janet the one who started the great artifact hunt at Fairfax last year?" asked Margaret.

"She's the one. Probably comes by it naturally. She's a descendant of Zebulon Pike, you know," Carolyn said.

"She thought she found a hidden panel in the passage to the north tower on the third floor," she continued. "A torn newspaper

Elizabeth Tidwell

article sticking out from behind a board mentioned a wedding; there wasn't even a date on it. Gail told her about the Langhorne locket, and Janet's excited screams brought girls running from all down the hall."

"What a mad search of closets and loose baseboards!" said Margaret. "They found a few buttons and even a small ring, I think. But no locket."

"Our students should apply themselves so rigorously to their studies," said Carolyn, reflecting that new scholastic honor societies and honor clubs for dramatic activities and speech already had stimulated excellence.

She noted that the musicians had a variety of opportunities, too. "Why, the Fairfax Chorus prepared twenty chorales and oratorios last year for programs at churches and the Woodrow Wilson Hospital. And the men's and women's clubs enjoyed popular music by the Dozinettes."

"The Boots and Saddle Club hunter trials and horsemanship shows were big hits," added Margaret. "Now what are we going to do about our sports teams?" she joked.

"I know. The faculty almost beat the students at the big baseball game last year," Carolyn, the second baseman, bragged. "At least the swim team had a very successful 'aquacade'. I like that name for the artistic swimming, and it was a big benefit for the March of Dimes and Red Cross."

"Maybe the aquacade will join our rich traditions here," Margaret said, panting at the brisk walk to the terrace. "The annual events and ceremonies build a rich camaraderie among the students, with their families, and as alumnae," she said with pride.

"My favorite is the senior ring figure, with the dads escorting their daughters all dressed in white and holding a dozen roses," she continued. "It's so beautiful, even in the gymnasium. Not exactly a debutante ball, like the Langhornes," she chuckled, "but certainly a beautiful rite of passage here."

"My favorite is the laurel chain ceremony," said Carolyn. "The seniors, in their white caps and gowns, carrying those long chains of flowers and greenery around campus and down to this little level place in front of the terrace." She recalled how, as the seniors joined in a circle, the juniors formed a ring behind them. Then the seniors passed the chain to them while singing the old song.

"I can't remember the words," she continued. "But they sing about pledging their love to each other, their pride in being Fairfax daughters, and passing the chain as a symbol of their faith and trust in each other."

"And they mean it," Margaret affirmed. "I've talked to many of our alumnae, and they cherish their time at Fairfax and its traditions."

"Hmmmmm," Carolyn said sleepily. "It's nice to be part of this place and of a grand country. Look! The porch lights are going out for the night and"—she turned—"so are the lights at Fairfax."

"We are out way past curfew," said Margaret, also with a yawn. "We need to get to bed so we can prepare tomorrow for the fall session before us and the opportunities to see the traditions of Fairfax and national honor continued."

"A bit much," said Carolyn. "But I concur with the general sentiment and challenge."

They hugged and walked across the slope and Reservoir Street to the faculty house.

Adelia kept Mollie on her leash as they walked through the back parking lot and into the arched passageway between two sections of the two-story brick building. The bricked up windows on the left revealed the south side as a later addition. The modern structure had been used at various times as freshman housing, a senior dorm, a junior college living area, and for science classrooms since its 1956 opening. Now it was another rental property in the complex.

"Oh, excuse me," said a young woman as she opened the door suddenly and fished in her pockets for quarters for the Coca-Cola machine, located incongruously, Adelia thought, in the outdoor hallway. "Oh, you have the cute little puppy. I've seen you walking it around."

"Hi. I'm Adelia, and this is Mollie. I live on the second floor of the main building."

"Hi, I'm Shirley. I live on the second floor of this building down on the corner near the gym."

"Do you mind if I ask you what it's like inside?" Adelia asked. "I'm scoping out all the buildings and grounds and doing research on Fairfax Hall at the library. I'm kind of a history buff and maybe a mystery writer someday."

"Why don't you come in? It's okay," Shirley said as Adelia hesitated. "The dog's fine."

"The structure was traditionally institutional, with walls a very light greenish color," Adelia mused, remembering the discovery that pea-green halls in hospitals make patients feel worse. Linoleum, like the floors in the main building, but none of the wainscoting and paneling. None of the shedding either."

"John lets us have a little kitchen here," Shirley said, opening the door on a refrigerator and counters of cookware and appliances scattered about. "Over there"—she pointed across the hall—"are old classrooms. Come on upstairs, and I'll show you my room, if you like."

"No grand staircase here," Adelia thought as they climbed uncovered cement steps to a plain hallway with rows of doors opening into rooms on either side. All of them were closed at the moment, adorned with an interesting array of signage.

Shirley opened her door into a one-room area with flowered quilt on a single bed and sheer curtains in the window. Several suncatchers gleamed there. The walls held a few posters and pictures over an inexpensive bookcase, a small dresser and two chairs. "Not much," Shirley said. "But it's home." She smiled.

"Our rooms aren't much different," Adelia said. "A few more touches in the hall and lots more deterioration in some of the rooms.

You'll have to come over sometime and see my place. Thanks for the tour, Shirley."

Completing the outside passageway, Adelia turned left at the end to glance into the classroom windows. Chairs, tables, and red cotton curtains were tossed about. She let Mollie off her leash and followed her up the five steps of irregular granite stones and mortar to the tennis courts.

The courts were cracked now, with ample moss growing in some crevices and tall grass in others. A few night crawler tracks still patrolled the surface. The near court was set up also for volleyball. All the nets were gone as was most of the side fencing. A weathered backboard stood stoically between the two courts. The remains of what appeared to be a gazebo were on the in-land side.

Farther back, a small glade was overgrown in skinny trees, shapeless bushes, and creeping vines. John said there were over fifty varieties of trees on the property, but Adelia was not into botanicals.

In the middle of the glade hunkered a three-sided outdoor grill; the fourth side was a chimney. The brick was well-worn and the iron bars obviously unused for some time.

Coming back along the in-land road, Adelia and Mollie passed the Paint Shop, so designated by its sign. The aggregate concrete walls were swirled on the outside with plaster in a similar manner to the gym. They surrounded only insulation batting—adroop from the ceiling—a small rusted fan high in the back, and the natural detritus accumulated by disuse and door open to the elements.

It was hard to believe, Adelia thought, that this property had once been a girls prep school of considerable public stature.

Chapter 13

"This is a wonderful place to relax under the stars," said the business manager, leaning back against the roof of the north perpendicular. "No glare from the city lights."

"Even better than the cupola," said the secretary. "But you have to be more careful about not falling off."

"Do you come up here often, Swann?" he asked. "What made you think about crawling out here on the roof?"

"Oh, the girls have been doing it for years. Of course, I don't officially know that, and neither do you, Harry Nash. Sometimes when I come out to join—er, catch them—they offer me a little hard cider as a bribe. They bring the cider up from the kitchen and let it ferment."

"Why, Miss Marks. I am shocked," he said mockingly. "Sounds like I better add some insurance coverage."

"That's right, Harry. You watch over the books, like a good business manager. And I'll help Miss Strother with the discipline." She chuckled.

"I really needed a break this evening after working on those grade reports and transcripts all day," she said. "Students and faculty have a summer holiday, and you and I get to finish up the old year and prepare for the next. I finally finished the last of the transcripts for the first-year junior college ladies for their new schools."

"It's really a shame we closed the junior college this year," said Harry. "But, Mr. Gates wants to concentrate on the finishing school. Probably a good idea with the changes coming in public institutions."

Swann stared at the sky. "Mrs. Ruhr says Mars will be the closest to earth in thirty-two years in early September. I have a hard time finding Mars, but there is Venus," she pointed proudly. "Of course, everybody knows how to find it since it came so close to the moon in March. Looked a lot closer than eighty-six million miles."

"It has been an astronomical year," agreed Harry, "starting with that sun spot bombardment in February. I heard the radio was in jeopardy when you and Marjorie lost the basketball game."

"That was nothing," said Swann. "I thought Janet Carter was going to throw her penny loafer right through the television set when we lost *I Love Lucy*. It was a good thing it didn't happen during Elvis Presley on *The Ed Sullivan Show*.

"We certainly had to be more vigilant in chaperoning the passion pit when the jukebox became the most reliable entertainment."

"The what pit?"

"Oh, Harry. Don't tell me you haven't heard of it!"

"I've done my share of watching to make sure I can see between couples when they're dancing in there," he said. "I was not aware of the name.

"Look, Swann. There's Leo just above the mountain, over the end of the Science Building," Harry said, carefully changing his position and pointing. He mentioned the dorm space provided in the new building, but said it was the chemistry, biology, and medical science labs that made the expense worth it.

"Just as we were recovering from the war years," he emphasized. "We can't replicate the experiments here, of course. But seeing scientists on television use electron microscopes and make rain and lightning in labs has generated a great deal of interest."

"I hear Miss Gambrill is trying to set up experiments next year using the principles of the new Swanson frozen foods," the secretary said, carefully picking her half-full Coca-Cola bottle out of the gutter. "And she ordered a model of the double-helix of DNA molecule."

"From the latest to the oldest. I received a supply request from Willy Lazton today for more iron rods," said Harry. "He only has two left since making the Class of Fifty-six chain link and grills

Elizabeth Tidwell

for the new rock fireplace behind the tennis courts. I don't know which was more exciting this spring—the traditional ceremony by the stable to add the link or the big barbecue at the grill.

"Willy is a real mountain man of the old school," he continued, accepting a cookie from Swann. "Hunts bear, runs a logging camp, butchers and cures meat—and shovels fuel for the boiler.

"I will never forget the day I saw him jump down into the pit behind the gym to put some order to a new train car load of coal. Kind of a modern day Davy Crockett without the coonskin hat and with a good number of black smudges."

"He's a bit um rough, but good to have around. I think the girls are afraid of him. But not nearly as much so as Joe, the night watchman," Swann said.

"Linda complained to me a few weeks ago that, if Joe catches them in the halls, he just stands there until they move into him," she explained. "Linda said the girls usually shut their doors until they hear him go by, carrying that huge ring of keys and pulling his bad leg behind him."

"They better be glad Joe hasn't caught them playing pranks," Harry said, ticking off incidents. "Let's see. There were the Coca-Cola bottles and the cherry bombs rolling down the hall. And something about plastic wrap on the toilet seats. And putting socks behind the clangers on the bells, although Mrs. Vance solved that by beating on a dishpan."

"I see you didn't list any flooding incidents," said Swann. "Someone told the girls the second floor slants so much and the linoleum is so wavy because past classes have had too many water fights. Is that true?"

Harry smiled. Swann decided to ignore his silence.

"Joe has failed to catch any of the Fishburne cadets—so far," she said. "Mrs. Pomer nearly nabbed the one on the third floor who played taps on the bugle. By the way, I hear the forty-five rpm records fit nicely into the crowns of the cadet hats for easy transportation and exchange."

She paused to finish her drink. "Joe should be able to smell the cadets with all that Old Spice. But the girls put it so liberally on their pillows that no one can be sure of the source any more."

"Second only to the scent of riding clothes shut up in the closet too long," chuckled Harry. "Karen asked me for an extra two dollars in her allowance one week last month so she could buy new vitamins. She left the top off the container which she stores on the shelf. Of course, I gave her a hard time about it, saying they were probably ruined from the smell of smoke on her clothes."

"I think the biggest stink was the skunk under the porch that closed the dining room for two days," Swann laughed.

"I'm afraid the smoking observation is all too true," she continued. "I walked into the second floor smoker not five minutes after study time last February and could not see a thing except an occasional hand reaching toward one of those red tin ashtrays. They don't have to worry about anyone cheating at bridge; they can barely see the cards in front of their faces."

"I was surprised when Mr. Gates started letting them smoke," Harry said. "I suppose it would be hard to stop it. At least, they have to have their parents' permission."

"Speaking of February. Do you remember when all the girls from Texas and Florida ran outside in that horrible hail storm?" asked Swann. "They thought it was snow."

"I suspect they were encouraged in that," Harry winked, but Swann did not see it in the darkness. "I remember having to order some new trays for the dining hall a month later after several were used to sled down the hill. I think they like that more than skating on the outdoor pool."

"The really nice event in February was the college ring figure," Swann noted appreciatively. "I'm always amazed at how the girls can decorate the gym so that it looks like a ballroom. What a sensational arch for the presentations and the big pink hearts everywhere.

"All those proud fathers trying to guide their daughters in the big hoops under waves of tulle and lace," she continued. "It was so nice of you to call Dupont and arrange for Mr. Ritter to get off so he could escort his daughter."

"Our own version of the debutante ball is one of the most popular traditions with the young ladies," agreed Harry, ignoring the compliment. "I guess the high school ring figure will step up a notch now, although it has always been very popular."

"I wonder if Nora was a debutante like her sisters?" Swann mused aloud.

"Nora who? Oh, you mean the youngest Langhorne sister. I don't know," said Harry. "She was said to be dreamy, disorganized and unschooled. But physically alluring and very kind-hearted. You know, she just died last year."

"Is that where you got the description—in the obituary?" Swann teased.

"No. I often read copies of the *Richmond Times-Dispatch*. And occasionally I read the society pages," Harry said, carefully shifting again.

"Did you see the story a couple of months ago on Jackie Marlinto, the May Queen in fifty-three?" Swann asked. "She went back to Lima and established Peru's first eye bank. And she's running a school for deaf children."

"I think the young ladies from Latin America get a very good education here," said Harry. "We have thirteen this year, and five from the Mideast."

"I often overhear whispered wonderment about the Cubans," said Swann, tapping her foot to a Latin beat in her mind. "The other students think them so rich and mysterious because they never talk about their lives there and where they get the money for such gorgeous clothes. Maybe that they are related to Castro and will be whisked away in the middle of the night."

"Well. . . ." Harry was mute again, then offered, "We have our share of well-to-do Americans. Kathy told me about taking Julie to New York over Thanksgiving break. Kathy's father is managing editor of *Good Housekeeping*, you remember. The girls saw *West Side Story* and the Rockettes and went shopping at Saks."

Harry wondered if he could safely reach his bottle of milk. "Julie is what the girls call an oil brat," he said, sighing with success. "She went to school in Saudi Arabia while her father was with ARAMCO, until high school. Then she decided, in all the world, to come here."

"I thought for awhile that she might date Barry Goldwater Jr.," said Swann. "Not enough dances with the Staunton Military Academy guys, I guess.

"Speaking of Nora Langhorne and Broadway musicals," she continued. "I thought we were going to get by a year without the annual Langhorne skit. Then along came *Brigadoon* and *My Fair Lady*, and the mystery of the locket struck again. Rather a strange combination of glee club and verse choir this year."

"Be glad they gave it a more academic twist than imitating *Gidget* with hula hoops!" replied Harry. "Or something as somber as *Long Day's Journey into Night*. Of course, I do not see the locket fitting into either of those."

"Well, we survived Donna's aunt taking all those girls to see *Love Me Tender* at the Wayne Theater," Swann said. "No telling how long it would take us to get that Elvis flick for Saturday night movies in the auditorium, if ever."

"And everyone enjoyed Mary's father bringing strawberries for the whole school," said Harry, his mouth watering with remembered taste. "That beat Sunday morning sweet rolls, juice, and milk at the top of the stairs for best culinary moment this year."

"Mary was even more surprised when he and her mother brought up that beautiful dress for her to wear for May Court. I think most of the court was surprised this year," said Swann. "That's a nice tradition, letting the parents do the shopping and preparation to surprise the honorees. There's such a buzz of activity among newly announced royalty as they gather in the Art Room before the ceremony."

"I think the biggest surprise this year was when Karen finally passed the swimming test so she could graduate," said Harry, carefully preparing to go back inside. "She spent three years in the shallow end of the pool with her paddle board. It took her well into the night last week to swim from one end to the other and back. Then everyone cheered."

"Hurray!" Swann shouted as he, not so gracefully, made it in the window. Harry helped her in anyway.

Seeking an unusual location, Adelia led the retreat group to what she called the cement pond for the second meditation. The Fairfax Hall outdoor pool was north of the main building, its derelict condition becoming increasingly apparent as the women walked down the uneven slope. Small trees grew in soil blown into the west end over the years, and plants and vines found purchase in cracks along the walls.

Members of the group straddled knee-high, nettle-like purple wildflowers as they sat on the slotted cement bench at the east end. Once the May Day court perched there properly and prettily in their pastel gowns, watching skits that accompanied the annual pageant. They were framed, stage-like, from the pool by the long graceful curve of a railing atop a balustrade of diamond-shape columns—all cement. The railing was deeply pocked now and steps into the pool were shattered into dangerous pieces.

Here, years ago, small canoes were paddled and students learned to swim and perform water ballets before the gymnasium was built. The west end was deeper until filled in, some said after a child drowned there. John claimed a ghost was connected to the tragedy, but Adelia could find no other mention of it. Now the pool contained only puddles of rain water, one deep enough to form a slight sandbar, cutting through the accumulated silt.

Once the pool was the center of outdoor grandeur. Today it served as a fitting backdrop for a lesson on the fragility of life's dreams.

Chapter 14

"Here, Becky. Sit down. Jane went to get you some dry clothes," the secretary said, leading the student into her office.

"Can't I just go up and change," Miss Marks. "I'm getting your couch all wet and. . . ."

"Don't worry about that," Swann said, focusing on the face, framed by dripping curls. "Sit here a minute, and let's talk."

"I just didn't get to him in time," she said shakily. "I walked into my room, and the window was open, you know, because it was a warm night. I thought I heard a splash and a little cry. I just dropped out the window and ran for the pool."

She paused at the surprised look on Swann's face. "I used to live on a farm. We dropped out of the loft all the time. Oh, Miss Marks, he was in the deep end and. . . ." She broke into deep sobs.

"You tried your best, Becky. Oh, thank you, Jane," she said. "Come hold this afghan up while Becky changes. Good, now go down to the kitchen and have Marcelles make a big mug of hot tea with a generous amount of warm milk. Thanks."

"Do you want the nurse to come check you over, Becky? What about calling your parents?" Swann said, worried about psychological effects.

"I think I'll be all right, Miss Marks. I'm just shaky now that it's over." She leaned back against a cushion. "Who was the little boy? He looked really young, maybe four or five."

"His sister was taking music lessons," Swann explained. "He must have wandered out of the gymnasium while his mother watched the girls work on the welcome party decorations."

"I can't believe he made it to the pool without falling over the wall into the thicket," Becky said, genuinely surprised.

"Yes, I need to speak with Mr. Nash about making sure parents adequately supervise their younger children while their siblings are taking lessons. And even those children after their lessons are over." She added that admonition to the upcoming discussion.

"Mrs. Handley uses the time during lessons to teach an adult how to read a few blocks away. That's very nice," she said. "But she got back a few minutes late a few days ago and couldn't find her daughter."

Swann realized too late that another incident would do nothing to elevate Becky's mood but decided she had to finish the explanation. "One of the girls took her daughter to the porch to see the spring bok statue the Scott family gave us from their trip to Africa. And they stopped to look at the new grandfather's clock in the parlor. That was nice, too, but it sure gave us a scare."

Her own need to practice the conversation obscured her focus on the present. "I know, as the business manager, Mr. Nash likes the extra income the lessons bring. But . . . well tonight shows what can happen."

"Oh," Becky sobbed again and waved off Swann's sympathy. "It's not just tonight. This has been such a horrible week." She blew her nose loudly.

"What else happened, Becky? Thank you, Jane," Swann said. "Would you like her to stay, Becky?"

"No, no thank you," she said, sipping gratefully from the mug while her friend looked on. "Jane, would you go up and tell Charlotte and Tina I'm all right. And Mrs. Alexander that I won't be in study hall. I'm supposed to study with Cynthia. . . ."

"It's all right, Becky," she replied. "I'll help her with math after I get your bed ready for an early night-night."

"Thank you, Jane," the secretary said. "Would you ask Dean Smith to check and see if the rest of the girls are all right. She may want to step into study hall or call floor meetings."

"Sure," said Jane, trying to be cheery. "See you a little later, Becky. Time for a hug."

"Now what else happened this week, Becky," Swann asked as Jane departed.

"Oh, my little sister, Susanna from Texas. She's just not doing well at all," Becky replied, sniffling. "I could tell when she came through the front door that it was going to be hard for her. She had to ride the bus up from some place called Corsicana by herself with all that extra luggage and get a taxi down at the station. I don't think she has ever been away from home before."

"Didn't she get the letter that Nancy wrote to all the new girls?" asked Swann. "Most of them say the letter prepares them for our expectations and gets them excited about the traditions."

"Oh, I know, Miss Marks," Becky said, beginning to explain. "But she's living in a dorm room with someone she doesn't know, when the first girl she really connected with is in the other wing, the new one, of the brick building." Her words rushed together.

"She's just scared, you know, of all the formality, and getting things right at dinner, and studying, and everything. I try to help, but . . . . Is it true they send the girls up from Texas to get culture?"

The question was serious, but Swann had to laugh. "Not all of them, Becky. We've had some beauty queens from there, and I believe one or two were first runners up in Miss America pageants later."

"It's just not easy for some girls," she continued. "I think you were one of the exceptions. You just jumped right in. Hmmm. Bad choice of words," Swann said after a long pause."

"Well, it helped getting to bring Happy Gal with me," Becky said with more understanding. "She loves the jumping courses and the hunts out at Shenandoah Farms. And, I think she likes Miss Fowler's horse, Virginia Gold, too. Not so much Tattle Tale, the new chestnut mare."

"Who's at the head of Susanna's table this month?" Swann asked.

"Jackie Douglas," Becky replied, coming to a sudden realization. "She's from Texas, too. Her dad was a lawyer for Jack Ruby.

"It's going to be an interesting month at that table," she continued. "Two of the others in that seating are diplomat's daughters. You know what a hard time their families had during the confusion after the Kennedy assassination."

"Tell you what, Becky. I will take Jackie's place for the next couple of nights and try to take some pressure off," said Swann. "I think Cindy has a birthday tomorrow. So Susanna will enjoy two of the fun traditions at supper with the happy birthday song and the individual birthday cake at that table. I'll see if Miss Miller will schedule fried chicken Saturday. Even Mrs. Lawler says—"

"In the south you may eat fried chicken with your fingers," Becky joined in. "Oh, that's the other thing. Susanna's napkin ring wasn't ready when she left Texas—the jeweler forgot to put on her initials—so she didn't have one until she got it in the mail yesterday." Swann considered how cute traditions can cause anxiety.

"She'll enjoy Mr. Nash's reading of the early copy of the *News-Virginian* comics Saturday night," Swann continued, stressing positive things. "And let's organize a blanket party on the front lawn for Sunday supper."

"Good idea, Miss Marks," Becky agreed. "Susanna will like the Sunday morning doughnut buffet, too."

"What else can we do?" Swann paused. "One thing, of course, would be to 'pamper'"—Miss Marks held her fingers up for the quote marks—"others who are having a hard time. Someone said Ginny had to borrow clothes because her suitcases were filled with winter things too heavy to send later."

"We always have a few girls who have that problem. Some townies come prepared with 'care' boxes"—Becky followed Miss Marks's lead—"with a few summer things.

"That's one problem Susanna doesn't have," she continued. "Her parents followed the required clothes list to the letter. And they sent up extra things with the napkin ring."

The words came tumbling out again. "She has a gorgeous yellow dress for the first dance at Fishburne next week. And you should see her puppy dog pajamas with matching robe. I don't know if House Mother Mouse—I mean Mrs. Taylor—will approve of the doggie face slippers, though."

"I believe Susanna will find her place at Fairfax Hall pretty soon," laughed Swann. "She has some background in speech, doesn't she?

"Yes. She won several competitions in eighth and ninth grade," Becky affirmed. "Her parents really debated"—she smiled at the pun—"about sending her this far away but thought she would get excellent training here, in music, too. Robin is already recruiting her for the Langhorne program. She wants to do some kind of Greek chorus thing." Becky rolled her eyes.

"Well that will be different," Miss Marks sounded just as doubtful. "I got the impression the Langhornes were much more er jovial than that, especially the father, Chillie. Maybe it can center on Lizzie, the postwar baby, who lived in Richmond during reconstruction."

"According to Robin, Nancy had her moments, too. Really into Christian Science and serious religious studies," Becky said. "And Phyllis was known for introspection and Nora for dreaming. There may be hope for this play yet."

"I understand you're in charge of decorating for ring figure, Becky. That's quite a job," Swann said, encouraging Becky further into happy expectations.

"Well, I don't think we can live up to the Taj Mahal theme with the elephant arch of fifty-nine. But Kay and Alice and I are coming up with good possibilities," she replied.

"Sarah was going to be on the committee, but she was selected to organize the May Court skit," she continued. "They're looking at a dance pageant, 'Around the World in Sixty Minutes'." She ticked off a list of tunes, including the French can-can, Russian Swan Lake, Hawaiian hula, a Viennese waltz, and a Near Eastern harem dance. "I doubt that Mr. Gates will allow only veils," she said with a broad grin.

"They're considering a colorful Latin number," she said quietly, "but Sarah is having a hard time after losing her boyfriend. You know she was seeing Rafis Levaton at Staunton Military Academy until he graduated last year."

Becky explained that he was the son of the dictator, Rafael Trujillo, and saw his father assassinated in the Dominican Republic while the cadets were watching television their freshman year.

"His cousin was a cadet at Augusta Military Academy for awhile," she added. "His girlfriend, Kim Novac, visited there pretty often. Sarah says she is real pretty."

"Well, I hope Sarah's senior experience improves as she gets into activities and meets new cadets at the dances," Swann said. "It's going to be an interesting year."

She paused, considering. "I'm sorry it's off to such a rough start for you, Becky. But, keep up the good work, and you'll be a contender for the Fairfax Hall Honor Medal. You've certainly demonstrated a spirit of loyalty to the ideals and traditions of the school in the last three years."

"Thanks, Miss Marks. I appreciate your very kind words—and your help talking this through tonight," Becky reached over and half-shook, half patted the secretary's hand. "It has really meant a lot."

"Enjoy the fun things, Becky." Swann gently held the hand in her two. "Cherish the dances, the outings to Williamsburg and Charlottesville, the tea with your class mother, the horse shows."

She leaned closer. "But I want you to know that you can always come back and visit with me," she said. "Let's listen to some World Series and basketball. You can always go out and watch sports on the new color television on the enclosed porch, but I like the radio."

"I will consider it an honor to enjoy the excitement of the wide world of sports with you, Miss Marks," Becky replied enthusiastically. "But I'll join the gang on the third floor watching the British bands on *American Bandstand*.

"I wish one of them—wouldn't the Beatles be fabulous. I wish one would come to the Paramount in Charlottesville," she continued. "It's such a great place with that gigantic thrust stage—I think that's what it's called."

She sighed, very tired from the night's adventure, but offered, "Perhaps you will join a few of us for some Saturday lunches at The Southern and the movies, Miss Marks. We will expect, of course, that you do a proper job of chaperoning us and safeguarding the reputations of ourselves and the school."

"Of course. I don't want you to jeopardize your chance at the medal, not to mention your privileges," Swann agreed, making a sudden decision. "Why don't you be the keeper of my favorite

Fairfax statement plaque this year." She retrieved it from atop a filing cabinet and handed over the framed calligraphy so that Becky could read it.

> The primary purpose of Fairfax
> Hall is to develop its students into the
> highest type of womanhood with
> appreciation of the true and beautiful
> in life. Joyousness of youth is encouraged;
> gracious living is emphasized,
> and the privileges and obligations of
> American citizenship are stressed.
> Our curriculum and activities encourage
> thoroughness in work, preservation
> of health and development of true culture.

"And take this one to Susanna," she said, lifting it off a shelf. "But you better wait until she feels a little more comfortable first."

Becky tucked the first into the crook of her arm and scanned the small, simply framed typed sheet:

> Expectations
> To be a lady in both speech and manner.
> To have sincere understanding and
> sympathy for all persons, no matter
> how divergent their backgrounds.
> To give constructive assistance to others
> by thought, word and deed.
> To have respect for the worthwhile aims
> and accomplishments of others.
> To diligently practice truth and honor,
> cooperation and consideration,
> friendship and loyalty, kindness and
> reverence.
> To use discretion in social behavior.

"Thanks, Miss Marks. We will try to live up to these," said Becky, growing teary-eyed again. "I'm going to put mine on my desk so I can see it daily, and so will everyone else who comes in to 'borrow' my pencils." She tried but could not raise her quote fingers.

Adelia and Mollie were enjoying a morning at the back of the property on the south side, an area with no structures. Adelia sat on a stump, about chair height, contemplating a return to the apartment for her camera. In front of her, a cluster of brilliant orange toad stools grew up around two cogs, about four inches in diameter, nestled low in green foliage. One lay fully on its side; the other balanced against it.

Mollie wandered toward the stable, and Adelia thought she better ensure Sean's large dogs were securely in the stall. Sean was a sometime resident of the third floor north perpendicular.

Moss richly carpeted the building's roof, and several louvers of its small cupola dangled. Otherwise, the structure looked sturdy. Walking under an arch of the front overhang, Adelia noticed for the first time a horseshoe embedded in the ground just outside the doors.

Inside to the left was a small room with face-high mirror where girls must have checked the set of their caps before entering the riding ring. Thirteen stalls—six on that side and seven on the other—were empty except for a few torn bales of hay and debris likely brought in by assorted wildlife. No horses boarded there now. In the corners, the half-basket shapes of rounded bars were empty. Holes remained ready above, but hay no longer filled the loft. Nor was there anyone to fork it down.

Adelia followed Mollie out the stable's other portal. A one-story structure with sliding barn-looking doors sat to the left. One was open just enough to see a yellow sports sedan from perhaps the fifties or sixties, minus its glass and well-coated with dust. Looking through an age-enlarged knothole on the other end, Adelia spied a stack of lumber, apparently piled there recently.

To the east of both buildings, an open door beckoned to a room half the size of a stall. Inside, a motley collection of metal and wood junk surrounded a tricycle resting on one pedal. The floor appeared to be raised, except further inspection revealed the end of another stable, a store room perhaps. Ground falling away from the foundation there made the entrance almost waist high.

This stable was larger, maybe the nicer one once. Now the ground was dangerously uneven along the central path and in the large stalls, nine on one side, eight on the other. Adelia assumed the story-and-a-half middle room was for tack, although none hung there now. The whole structure was ready to collapse.

From talks with former students, Adelia knew the opportunity to bring their horses and get additional equestrian training was a key deciding factor for Fairfax Hall over other prep schools. There was nothing to commend the riding facilities now.

Chapter 15

"Whoo! That was fun," Ellen said, grabbing two Dr Peppers from the cooler and collapsing into one of the green, slotted lounge chairs on the side porch.

"May the friendships formed at Fairfax live throughout the years." Laura, took one of the bottles and raised it to clink against Ellen's. The effort required to lead a snake chain of students hand-in-hand through the building and out on the back lawn was worth it, she thought. "We're off to a good year," she said aloud.

"We had to almost lasso the juniors at the end of the second floor," Ellen complained. "But they sang 'Loudly praise our alma mater, best school in the land' so enthusiastically the sophomores filed right in from the other side. Even the freshmen came pouring out of the Science Building to join us."

"I think they were just happy to get out of there, Ellen. They keep the freshmen holed up for the first six weeks. Those dorm rooms are nicer, but the building's so plain," said Laura. "Whatever do they do without our nooks and crannies and the challenge of keeping pencils and Chapstick on the desks."

She leaned over conspiratorially. "We'll make things more interesting around Halloween. We need some special effects when Sandy tells the story of the ghost at the window near the top of the gym."

"You're incorrigible, Laura," Ellen humphed. "You better watch it, or we'll lose our senior privileges. I want to make lots of trips into town this year."

Elizabeth Tidwell

"You mean, no shaving cream and confetti in the business office and no water bucket set over the door to surprise Mamma Billows," Laura gasped mockingly. "And I so wanted to try swimming in the reservoir tank up the hill."

"I think we need to give Mrs. Billows a break this year," said Ellen seriously. "I saw her coming down from the third floor two nights ago, backward. Sharon says she's inebriated—on cough syrup."

"Hmmmmm. Speaking of Sharon. She and Alex are already planning the Langhorne skit. That idea is getting so old." Laura stretched out the "so" and rolled her eyes. "Let's suggest a talent show with the locket as a theme," she said merrily. "People can draw pictures of it, write poems, sing songs. . . ."

"How, Laura? We don't even know what it looked like," said Ellen, feeling her exasperation at the end of a long day.

"That will make it even more fun. People can add their own romance," Laura replied enthusiastically, the ideas tumbling out. "A shadow box showing the location of the locket. A skit about opening the trunk at Mirador that Christmas after the honeymoon. It could have the locket and other items found by Nanaire and Nancy after the wedding. A quintet singing to represent the sisters. Better make it a quartet. Lizzie was never involved."

"How do you know so much about the Langhornes?" asked Ellen.

"Actually I'm a distant cousin," Laura said. "I also ran into some information on them while I was working to read every book in the library, including those big leather-covered ones. Oof!"

"How is that coming, by the way? You don't have much time left," Ellen admonished.

"A whole year!" Laura said righteously. "But you're right. There are so many things to do this year which conspire against my freshman-promise project." She liked the sound of that. "There's riding. Linda asked me to do big calligraphy sheets for ring figure. I want to learn some modern dance. And who knows what being vice-president of the class will entail."

"I hope your tenure goes better than Jo's last year. She had to work with Dean Lawter to expel those eight girls for smoking pot.

And those horrible two days when Katie and Tina disappeared with the two town guys, driving up to Front Royal." Ellen shuddered at the misery caused.

"That's the saddest thing, Laura—this sixties culture. Of course, it's late sixties at Fairfax, 1970 this year," Ellen said in a resigned tone. "One of those boys had a giant afro and the other a foot-long pony tail." She noted the increasing number of girls from homes where parents just want to get rid of them. "For a few, it's Fairfax or jail," she added.

"Fortunately, we still have a reputation good enough to attract Pearly Underwood and Louisa Lay," said Laura. "I just hope we don't recognize too much deviled ham and Bush's baked beans on Saturdays."

"Do you remember when Sylvia came back from Christmas break last year with the Pocahontas cameo passed down through their family?" Ellen asked.

"Then there's Lyn to whom we owe many thanks for the lighted tennis courts," she said, savoring one of the last sips of pop. "Didn't take long after her father visited here last year."

"What about Rikki Woodsby?" asked Laura, twirling her bottle and recounting Rikki's commercial for Southern Department Store and performance at the hospital. "I predict her singing and song writing will take her far. You know she came here after seeing an advertisement in *Vogue*."

"I didn't realize we were that upscale," Ellen said. "But it makes sense. We attract people from big city society, and Virginia girls choose us over Stuart Hall and St. Anne's."

"We still have the diplomats' daughters and people in the ruling classes who are their friends," she added. "What about Isabella from El Salvador? What a shoe freak!"

"More girls are coming from around here, though," Laura noted, proclaiming they had to do something special for Leora and Shawnee. "Remember the end of last summer when Hurricane Camille came over the Blue Ridge and practically wiped out Nelson County?" she asked.

"Leora's parents stepped off the porch and began running for higher ground just as their house began to go," she warmed to the tale and the words rushed out. "Logs were piled thirty feet high along David Creek. It usually has water only a few inches high. They lost almost everything. Fortunately, Leora was already here."

"And you know this because?" Ellen asked.

"I read the newspapers in the library from Charlottesville and Richmond last year," Laura replied, matter-of-factly. "And Leora has an anniversary copy of the *Nelson County Times*. I was in the lounge when she brought it in. She's just devastated, remembering it all over again."

Ellen nodded. "Shawnee told me that her aunt and uncle and cousins went to the attic as the water rose around Lovingston. Then the house broke apart." Her telling was slower. "Shawnee's aunt washed up along a hillside a mile from her yard, and her uncle wound up in a tree. They never found her two cousins."

They sat is silence for a moment before Laura asked, "Do Leora and Shawnee ride?"

"I think so, although not real well," Ellen replied.

"Why don't we ask them to ride with us out to Sunset Ranch tomorrow after classes," Laura said. "We'll take it real easy.

"We'll have to get permission from Miss Parker and Dean Lawter since they're not seniors," she continued, thinking through the logistics. "Miss Marks will help us."

"A simple ride would be nice, Laura. You can't always be practicing those intricate pinwheels and round offs for the horse shows," Ellen teased. "And Leora and Shawnee will be so glad to get out of that indoor donut riding ring."

"That is so aptly named." Laura stressed the third word. "Just like, I mean, naming a girl's school for Lord Fairfax, one of the biggest misogynists in Virginia. Where did that come from? I guess because he owned all this land." Laura was on her soapbox. "But the ring is definitely a donut, walls on either side of the circle path.

"That makes it so scary for inexperienced riders," she continued in a tone packed with incredulity. "There's no place to get clear if something goes wrong. The discipline of getting the hands just right and sitting the horse properly—that's critical in our competitions. But not scaring the new riders to death. 'Here lies Sally. She died in a donut.' Geez!"

"That would be something to bring up at President's Council," Ellen suggested. "Now that we have more room with the McGahey property, maybe they can put the beginners in a semi-enclosed outdoor ring for awhile and use the indoor ring for bad weather."

"A really good idea, Ellen. But I don't know how many improvements the Gates family will make," Laura said. "I'm hearing rumors about the school closing in a few years. It's hard to keep up high cultural standards nowadays."

Ellen tipped her bottle up for the last drop. "Did you notice they changed the statement in the handbook. More about personal interests and talents, natural endowments, maximum growth of the individual, and flexible curriculum."

"Signs of the times, I suppose," Laura shrugged. "I'm amazed at how liberal government class is this year. And, Mrs. Binger has already assigned an essay in English about how we view the hippie counter culture.

"Remember last year when so many of the girls took sides, north versus south, during the race riots in Washington, D.C.?" she asked sadly.

"I guess they're getting us ready for college," Ellen said, suddenly reflecting as much about a spot on her tennis shoe than changes in curriculum and culture. The spot reminded her how the whole senior class dyed their tennies red and put them in the dean's office just before graduation last May. The new dean always wore red Keds, and she took away almost all senior privileges.

"Yoohoo. Earth to Ellen!"

"Oh, sorry. I was just thinking about. . . . Never mind." She continued her ideas about educational quality. "Most of the new teachers are from the prestigious schools like Wellesley. And they have masters degrees rather than the B.A and B.S. degrees in public schools. That's why some of the townies come here."

"Oh, you mean it's not for the library?" Laura asked with a big smile. "I went down to the dedication of the new library in Waynesboro last year. . . ."

"Of course," Ellen nodded.

Laura ignored the jab. "Do you realize that the first librarian became a missionary and was the mother of the wife of Billy Graham?"

"Could not possibly live without that fact," Ellen mocked.

"I'm all for learning about the rest of the world," she continued. "But I'm looking forward to continuing traditions. Beth Ann and I have been talking about the synchronized swimming show. She wants to do 'A World of Color'."

"I'm sure, you'll explain the porpoise." Laura smiled at the play on words about the team's name. "I still can't believe you went from beginning swimmer to getting the most advanced swimming award last year. Completing all the Red Cross classes in only two semesters—was that some kind of record?"

Ellen struggled to rise from the sloping chair, plunging straight ahead to a straddle position, not from the side. "Like a fish out of water," she said before Laura could comment.

"Here's to traditions," Laura said as they clinked their empty pop bottles together. "I wonder how much trouble I'll be in with Elvin if I start a contest to see who can stick the most butter pats to the ceiling."

Ellen rolled her eyes. "He will dress you down big time. The black waiters have as much pride in proper behavior as the whole rest of the staff."

"Well, perhaps I can get away with just one little thing tonight," Laura smiled. "I simply have to have a frozen Milky Way, and it's almost time for lights out."

"If you're not careful, you're going to wind up in the infirmary from all these sweets," Ellen teased. "Maybe you could sneak around and find out why they never put anybody in the room over the kitchen."

"You're the big snoop," Laura said and gasped, "Ohhhh! That is so cold," as she slipped the candy bar under her blouse.

"Yoohoo! Is anyone here?" cried a female voice loudly from the entrance hall.

Adelia made it to the top of the stairs before the voice sounded again. "Hello, hello."

"Coming. I'm coming," Adelia said, beginning the descent.

"There she is," Gerald said haltingly, leaning heavily on the woman's arm. "There's Adelia. I told you about her."

"Yes, Father. How do you do, Adelia. I'm Lisa."

"Glad to meet you, Lisa. Would you like to sit down, Gerald? And you, too, of course. I can go upstairs and get ice tea," Adelia said. "I already have some made."

"Oh, thank you. But no, we can't stay long," Lisa said quickly. "Father told me how nice you have been to him."

"Well, I hope we didn't, er, overdo on his last trip," Adelia said, looking with concern at the obviously less fit man before her.

"Oh, no, Adelia. I was okay then." Gerald's reply was rapid but not hearty. "My health has deteriorated badly since I got a cold this summer. I had pneumonia, you know."

"I'm very sorry to hear that, Gerald. But I'm glad you came by today." Adelia was genuinely happy.

"I wanted Lisa to see this place," Gerald said, looking apologetically at his daughter. "I bore her talking about it all the time."

"That's okay, Father," she said, patting his hand gently. "It certainly is impressive. Father told me to go down to the ballroom to see if anyone was there." Lisa chuckled. "I think he just wanted me to see it."

"I'm glad you had the opportunity. You'll. . . ."

"Have you found out anything more about the locket, Adelia?" Gerald asked impatiently.

"Not a word. It's not mentioned in the Langhorne materials," replied Adelia. "And there's not much information about the hotel after the wedding. With all the renovations over the years, I'm surprised no one found it."

"Maybe there, well maybe there isn't a locket," said Lisa. "I mean, Father, you don't know anything specific about it, do you?"

"No, not really." The old man's head hung toward his chest. "I just feel such an attraction to this place. I hoped we could solve this little mystery." He leaned forward, and Lisa helped him up.

"I'll keep working on it, Gerald," Adelia promised. "Why don't you give me your number or an address where I can reach you. I may find something yet."

"Oh, I appreciate it, but. . . ."

"Here's my card, Adelia." Lisa rushed to pull it from her purse. "Let us know."

"Can we go down here a minute?" Gerald pointed down the office wing hallway.

"Sure. Sure I guess that's okay. Isn't it, Adelia?"

"Fine. Not much to see, but no problem."

Gerald walked steadily toward the end, looking resolutely ahead. He paused at the closed door of the dumbwaiter and at the back stairway, and stared for several minutes at the last door on the left.

"No, no . . . that's not it," he mumbled. "His steps were slower as he retreated to the foyer. Almost to the entrance, he looked up over the parlor door.

"Stopped at ten 'til ten. I wonder why."

"Let's go, Father," Lisa urged. "We need to get home. Thanks for everything, Adelia."

As they left, a cold chill entered the door, a reminder that winter was on the way.

Chapter 16

"I can't believe it's over," Helen said, standing on the front terrace and looking around at the people and May Day skit props. "Look. Even the May Pole streamers are drooping. There will never be another school like Fairfax."

"At least we sent it out in great style," said Linda with effort to have a cheery tone. "Miss Cohn said they were expecting one hundred fifty alumnae and friends. We have graduates in every state and thirty-one foreign countries, you know."

"She spent so much time with the riding drill team. We looked so grand in the horse show this spring, if I do say so myself," she continued, the words rushing out in great strides. "I sold her TGIF. I know she'll take care of him, and I can't take him to Sweet Briar next fall. I don't know what will happen to Old Jack, Buck, and Angelo though."

"The last *Chain and Anchors* was bittersweet," Helen said, still wrapped up in misery. "That passage from Ecclesiastes!"
  A time to kill
 And a time for healing.
  A time to break down
 And a time to build up.

"Now, there's the words to anchor our hearts and memories to Fairfax Hall." She seemed confused and sat down suddenly on the grass. Linda joined her, picking at stems of clover while trying to emphasize a brighter side.

"I like that the yearbook was dedicated to everyone, including the kitchen and cleaning staff. But especially to the Gates and Nash families and Miss Marks," she said, then looked up suddenly.

"I wonder if Mr. Gates knew about the closing when he read *A Christmas Carol* last year. We were so happy, seated all up and down the stairs to take part in the tradition."

Helen reminded her that there was a party for the cooking and wait staff's children, until the seventies. "My sister said it was so much fun seeing their bright eyes and hearing their squeals of delight when the girls handed them stockings off the mantle."

"My cousin told me about another Christmas tradition," Linda said. "The girls exchanged little gifts each day for a week and then more expensive presents at a big bash just before break. That link party was another way of emphasizing the enduring friendships forged at Fairfax."

"That must have been the start of our Christmas secret pals," Helen said. "Too bad we lost the symbolism."

"I was so surprised when Alicia was my secret pal this year," she added. "Her card just said to hold the piece of paper up to a candle. She wrote it in invisible ink."

"That's Alicia," Linda chuckled. "All that private investigation stuff. She even took PI classes so she could look for missing persons. I was down at the mailroom when she got her certificate of completion," she said, patting Helen's shoulder to bring her back from a silent reverie.

"I thought my Little Sister was going to go missing," Helen said, stretching out her legs and remembering the first day for her freshman charge. "After Karen got everything checked in and everyone admired her Indian-style bedspread and curtains, we went down to see her parents off. Half an hour later she was still sitting on the steps saying, 'What have I done?'

"I finally took her to get an ice cream bar on the back porch," Helen continued. "And, I made her my famous peanut butter sandwiches after study hall for a week. Now she has to find another school. She's devastated."

"Everyone is, even those of us who are graduating in a couple of weeks," said Linda, crossing her legs and leaning forward. "It's hard to believe we got through the spring session at all after that terrible assembly February thirteenth. Just before the Valentines Dance." Her voice turned bitter.

"I can't believe Mr. Nash announced the closing with not so much as a preamble—steadily rising costs, declining enrollment. Oh pooh!"

"Well, the dorm rooms in the science building were closed, and so was the perpendicular wing," Helen offered as an explanation. "I sneaked in there last week. The rooms are full of abandoned trunks and teddy bears and a bunch of those ugly green tables.

"I never did get into the cupola." She frowned at another dream ended.

"They can add my fake fur bedspread to the piles," Linda said more cheerily than the words implied. "I guess it's too hard to get enough students. We only had seven freshmen this year." That was a telling statistic, she thought.

"At least they relaxed the rules a bit," Linda continued, citing the cab rides to Pizza Hut rather than walking to Anderson's Market down the hill. "I thought that squeaking door to the arcade underneath was going to drive me nuts. You could hear it all spring when we took the Sunday suppers on the hill."

"I could have done with fewer rules on dating," said Helen, reaching unconsciously for her ex-boyfriend's ring, no longer hanging around her neck. "All those special rules and not being able to go off campus." Officially, she thought.

"Georgia has dated that guy from UVa for four years." Helen tried not to betray her jealousy. "He comes over every weekend, and Georgia is so embarrassed about all the regulations. She says she's going to marry him."

"At least, as a Fishburne cadet, Debbie's beau was more used to the rules," Linda replied. "Remember when she and Barbara worked so hard on the dance and didn't have dates; then two extra cadets showed up. Debbie came back to the room that night and told me, 'He's the one I'm going to marry.' And she is."

"Lots of rules and regulations," Helen sighed. "But we got to ride that night in the fresh snowfall and went all the way out to Keswick for the spring fox hunt.

"The outing to Woodberry Forest was different and fun," she continued, gaining enthusiasm. "I actually made it through the ropes course and discovered I really like camping."

"Sometimes I just enjoy sitting in the window seats of the arch over the portecochere. What an old-fashioned term," Linda said quietly. "It's also nice to sunbathe on the porch roof. With no one in the 'bridal suite' this year"—Linda motioned the quotes with her fingers—"the door's supposed to be locked. But it isn't hard to get in."

"Tammy and Lana planned to live there but were moved down toward the south end." Helen grinned, recalling their revenge. "Remember when they flooded the second floor—almost two inches deep—and it ran down the stairs into the parlor.

"Katrina was in the office making a phone call when one of the freshmen came in to tell Miss Marks that Dean Bruger needed her in the foyer right away," she continued, tears beginning to run down her cheeks at the thought of it. "When Katrina hung up and went out there, the dean was just standing with her hands on her hips, and Miss Marks was trying very hard not to laugh. I can't believe they got away with it."

"Oh, I think Jane had to make a number of laps to the front gate and back," Linda said smiling at the memory and rising to her feet. "And, as I recall, Tammy got in a lot of extra swimming practice for the 'Time in a Bottle' Porpoise show."

"I think Betsy is going to write a special poem for graduation," said Helen, whose look indicated mischief was expected. "Do you think they will erase her new one in the south turret room? It's the only commemoration this year of the fabled Langhorne locket."

She accepted Linda's hand up.

"I doubt it, unless the new tenant paints over it." Linda shook her head while relating rumors of a hotel, a home for senior citizens, or a police academy. "I don't know if anyone will buy it. My room slants so far to the front that my pencils roll off the desk."

"Memories will always linger 'round our school so dear," Helen began singing suddenly. Linda grabbed her hand and joined in.

Memories Will Always Linger

May the friendships formed at Fairfax
Live throughout the years.

Loudly praise our Alma Mater
Best school in the land.
Through the years we're friends forever.
Loyally we stand.

Suddenly the lights went out. And the radio. And the computer.

"Oh, phoo!" Adelia said to a dozing Mollie. "It's a good thing I saved that last edit." It was still light outside, though the natural illumination would fade quickly this dreary, rainy, cold afternoon.

She clicked on the leash and took Mollie downstairs to see what happened. At the pool room door, she met Tilley, Daly and her husband, George, and Sean. They already had beers and chips in hand.

"What's up?" Adelia asked.

"Don't know. Probably a transformer or something," said Tilley. "Maybe John will know when he gets back from checking pipes in the other building."

"Brrrrrr," John sounded with extra vibrating of his lips as he came in the back door. "Oh, great. The lights are out here, too. Has to be something on a wire around here." He retreated several steps to the equipment room to retrieve a flashlight.

"All the electricity is out, except a yard lamp over there," he reported, sweeping his hand presumably toward a house across the street to the south. "It probably has a solar battery—a long-lasting one."

Handing the light to Tilley and shrugging off his soaked hooded jacket, John said, "Let's get the generator, George, and hook it up to the refrigerator so everyone can put stuff in it if the electricity's out too long. I'll get the big lantern upstairs so we can play some pool while we wait. Tilley, can you get the kerosene heater going? I'm freezing."

"I think I'll walk Mollie, then grab a flashlight and do some exploring upstairs," Adelia said. No one commented on her snooping. She wanted to check the armoire and several areas of the second wing north perpendicular. "By the way, has anyone seen the guys from the third floor?"

"Off doing something down near Martinsville this weekend," said John, opening the door to the wing's back stairway. "Supposed to be in tomorrow night. Don't see them much."

"Neither do I. And I don't hear them a lot either after the big music bash a few months ago," said Adelia.

"Yeah. We all heard that," said Daley. "But I guess you got the most of it."

"Actually, they let some friends stay there while they were away. The buddies were pretty drunk when I went up to check on them," said John. "Too bad the real spirit didn't get them.

"Yeah, there's supposed to be some kind of ghost up there," he said, noting Adelia's quizzical look.

* * *

The armoire was sturdily built but not a fine piece of furniture. There was nothing in the drawer at the bottom and no hidden compartments revealed by her rapping at likely places.

Most of the doors along the hall were open. However, one in the middle, on the inner side was closed. As Adelia opened it, a cold draft blew out from an open window. As she crossed to shut it, she spied the strange attachment on the wall.

What else could she call it? About the size of a standard pillow, but more elliptical and irregular, it clung just beneath the window sill. Adelia didn't want to get too close in the dark room. The flashlight beam caught the edges of hundreds of shell-like petals, but thinner—like paper.

"What's that?" Daly said as she came through the door and flipped on the light switch. "Electricity's back. Wow!" The nest was less scary in full light, but not as beautiful.

"John needs to look at that," she said. "It should be too cold for wasps, but he better make sure."

"If they're gone, that'll make a great show and tell for Joy at school," Adelia said. "It's gorgeous."

"Find anything?" Daly asked.

"Not really," Adelia replied. "Hey. Want to go to the attic? I need to check out the top stair just below the cupola. It sounds hollow."

"I . . . I don't know, Adelia. You know, I'd never been up there until with you and Gerald. And then he fainted." She hesitated. "I heard the story of the ghost before."

"Come on," Adelia drew out the second word. "You can do it. I may need someone to hold the flashlight."

Higher in the building, light was still creeping through cracks in the roof. Not a good sign, Adelia thought. Daly shined the flashlight beam upward as Adelia climbed the stairs and then followed her. Adelia took the flashlight and played its beam carefully around the three visible sides of the top stair. Then she reached around behind.

"Yech," she screamed and reached for Daly as her companion seemed to lose her balance. "It's okay. Just a spider web." She took off her light sweater jacket and used it to rub the back of the stair before feeling more closely. Nothing unusual.

"That's it," Adelia said. "I've looked everywhere I can get into. The only treasure I found was a playing card and a little plastic heart inside the window seat on the third floor."

Chapter 17

The night watchman walked across the porte-cochere and driveway to the flagpole terrace to enjoy the spring night with a quick smoke, not at all surprised to see the Department of Correction's academy manager there. "A beautiful evening, Colonel Gessar. Looking forward to the weekend?"

"I sure am, Davey. "Three more weeks and we're done. This new group is something else. I can't get them to bed at night and I can't get them up in the morning. The women are crying because they are homesick and miss their children. The men are bored, but I can't get any of them to go rappeling with me up on the Blue Ridge.

"Captain Solder says the security officers gripe about the marching drills on the tennis courts," he continued. "And the counseling group complains about the heat in the classrooms. The only thing they all like is the food."

"No way they can complain about that," said Davey. "The academy is known for having the best food in Virginia."

"That's the one thing I hope doesn't change when we move into the new facility in Goochland," the colonel affirmed, but quickly repented from his condemnation of the rest. "We've had to work hard to make this site suitable for classes and drills. But it does have a lot of character."

"Like clanging pipes and creaking floors and the turkey buzzards circling from sundown to dawn?" Davey replied.

"Of course. And our extra visitors."

"You mean the ladies of the evening?"

"Davey!"

"It's true," said Davey, horrified at the reaction. "They come across the lobby like they're living here."

"Then why haven't you reported them to me before?" the colonel said harshly.

"Well . . . uh. What extra visitors do you mean?"

"Why the ghosts, of course," Gessar replied. "One of the nurses in the north wing awhile back said a woman spirit walked up and down outside her door almost every night. And a visitor returning from the bathroom saw her, too."

Davey nodded, taking care to thoroughly grind out the cigarette with his shoe and pick up the butt. "I'll never forget my first night shifts here. Everybody was in bed, but I thought I heard someone walking around several times."

He paused a moment to savor the smell of wisteria. "One night at two a.m. I heard footsteps coming down the main stairs and they stopped at the front door. Larry said the same thing happened to him."

Noting the colonel's interest, he continued. "The second time I saw one was near the stairs on the north end of the third floor. I wasn't afraid of it. It just seemed kind of mischievous. I walked about twenty feet toward it, and it evaporated."

Gessar nodded. "Captain Gooden told me a week after he started here what he discovered one real quiet evening. He says you can hear ghosts talking and laughing on the second and third floors, especially in the big lounge on the north end of the third."

"Who do you think they are? Uh, what do you think it is," the watchman asked.

"I don't know, Davey. One of the cooks—These local women know all the stories. Some of them have family that have worked here for generations," Gessar said. "Anyway, she said it's a housemother who always wore hats with veils."

He added that one of the students claimed to see that one. "Scared him so much he didn't get any sleep and that's why he couldn't get up for flag raising in the morning." The colonel rolled his eyes but nodded slightly as if that was a novel excuse at least.

"I think I saw that one, Colonel, going up the back stairs to the north second floor," Davey said. "A mist was forming in the shape of . . . . Well it had a gown down to the ankles, and she turned around and looked at me. But I couldn't really see her face. She was there about two minutes."

"That's pretty speci . . . well, it sounds like maybe you've been thinking too much about it, Davey."

"Oh, no, Colonel," the watchman protested. "I mean, I follow the same routine every night. Every hour I make a tour through the main lobby. It's always friendly and comfortable. And, then I go to the dining room. And it feels fine, too. But when I walk down the first floor hall near the offices and classrooms. Well, I don't know how to describe it." He lit another cigarette.

"Probably jitters in a very old building," the colonel mumbled, but said, "You remember, I had my own little experience last year. I was sound asleep, and about one a.m. I thought I heard you coming to tell me there was some kind of problem. But it sounded like high heels coming toward the door." He looked at his watch and at the cigarette.

"I was waiting for you to knock, but you never did. When I opened the door, no one was there. When I went downstairs to check, you were just coming in the back door."

"I remember," said Davey. "It wasn't too long after that student from Powhatan Prison came running downstairs in her underwear saying she saw something white and hanging in the air. Now that was a sight in itself."

"Have you ever seen the ghost in the window at the top of the gym? Or the one down by the pool?" Gessar asked.

Davey noticed the colonel was continuing the conversation even though the time to start security rounds had passed. "No. I've never seen one outside the main building." He shuffled his feet, trying to decide whether to leave or stay.

"I think things will be better when we move to Goochland next month," Gessar said thoughtfully. "We'll lose the ghosts in the brand new facility, and the students will be closer to their families."

Even though they will stay on campus, he thought, it will be easier for them to concentrate on policies and procedures, interaction, supervision of inmates, hostage response, and all that in modern classrooms.

"I'll miss sounding reveille and the national anthem from the cupola," he admitted aloud. "But I don't think I'd ever get used to firing practice at those paper silhouettes in that gymnasium. It's—well—it's kind of like a church with that cathedral beam ceiling forty feet high."

"It's really a shame the academy is moving after all the money the state spent upgrading to code and redoing the sprinkler system," said Davey.

"But the rooms are in very basic shape, at best," Gessar replied. "Students on the second floor, just off the lobby, are always griping about their pencils and pens rolling off the desks. Geez. They're always complaining. The DOC ought to sell them pencil holders.

"If you're not one of the first up for your morning shower, there's no hot water left," he continued. "Or too many people flush the toilet at once and you get scalded. And you have to stand in the cafeteria line forever for breakfast."

Davey raised his left eyebrow, and the colonel noticed.

"Adding the sidebars with fruit and cereal helped that," the academy manager said more positively. "I don't think there's any way we'll get the fantastic chow. Those Taco Tuesdays for lunch." The colonel licked his lips. "Even at the mid-morning and mid-afternoon breaks—nice platters of fruit, croissants, and ice cream."

Davey thought about his next statement a minute and decided it was safe. "Sometimes I pick up pieces of leftover fruit, sometimes crackers, and leave them out for the groundhogs and squirrels. No sense them going to waste," he added to cover his tracks in case that was against the rules.

"From what Mr. Nash says, there's always been a tradition of great food here," he continued, "at least since the beginning of the Fairfax Hall prep school years. Served with real style."

Gessar gazed at the cupola. "What's going to happen when we leave, Davey? Have you heard? Are you still going to have a job—that is if you want one when we're not here to guard you from the spirits," he chuckled.

"Yeah, I'll get to stay on. They need someone to keep an eye on the place," Davey replied. "I haven't finished nearly all the interesting books in the library. And I want to do some more checking in the crawl space under the middle wing."

"You're really into ground hogs and feral cats, are you?" Gessar was amused.

"Oh, there's more," said Davey enthusiastically. "There's a chest of drawers down there, but it's nailed shut. And I can't get it up through the little access hole. I don't know if I have the nerve to go back down in there."

"I could teach you some hand-to-hand combat," Gessar offered. "But I doubt it would do any good, especially if you interrupt a meeting of the spirits."

He shifted topics. "Isn't there a rumor about some kind of locket lost here?"

"There sure is. I've even used a metal detector outside." And inside—Davey did not want to admit that, perplexed as he was by scores of DOC rules and regulations. "I've found gold rings and necklaces, but no locket. And the state crews were all over this building—shoring up walls, rewiring, and replumbing before the academy moved in. I doubt there's any place left to look." Except that dresser, he thought.

"Speaking of hand-to-hand combat," Davey said. "Those town kids are going to miss your karate classes on Saturday mornings. And the ladies down at Lynn's Pancake and Steak House are going to miss Captain Solder's handlebar mustache."

"I'll miss the smell of beeswax as Betty cleans the breakfronts in the dining hall and all the beautiful wood paneling," Gessar replied. "And, I'll gladly miss the skunks down by the stables." He started walking back toward the building.

"Sometimes they make it up here, too." Davey trotted a few steps to catch up. "We may not have so much of a problem, though, when Mr. Nash gets the next group in here. He's talking to the local law enforcement people about training attack and drug sniffing dogs in the building and outside. There's lots of good places."

"I kind of hope the dogs don't last too long though," he continued. "It'd be nice to see the deer come back down the mountain."

He noted that they often ran and jumped on the front lawn until the traffic picked up with the student cars. "And their favorite eating is the moss down by the fuel oil tank. Just as good to them as your tacos."

Adelia tested the main doors to the church then went around to see if anyone was in the office, as marked by a sign on the side street. She used the heel of her hand to give a substantial knock. In a couple of minutes, a young woman dressed in jeans and a sweater came to the door.

"I'm Adelia, and I live up at Fairfax Hall," she introduced herself. "I've gotten really interested in the place and the girls' school. I understand that almost all the students attended church here."

"Hi. I'm Sharon," she responded, inviting Adelia down the hall to a Sunday School classroom for young grade schoolers, where she was working on some lesson sheets. "The school closed before I came here but I've heard about it. You ought to talk to Sheila, the church secretary. She's been here a long time and could probably tell you a lot."

"I hate to keep you from your work," Adelia apologized. "But do you think we could go into the main building a minute so I can see what the auditorium looks like?"

"Sure. Let me get the keys."

They walked then from the church office through a room with tables covered in pots and pans and spice containers. "This is a mess. We're remodeling the kitchen, just through there. But I thought you might want to see it," said Sharon. "Apparently the school held some pretty big dinners here."

"That's interesting," mused Adelia, aloud. "They had their own industrial-size kitchen and beautiful dining room." Then she remembered a former student describing church suppers and the Fairfax girls taking plates heaped with cake back to the dorms."

Adelia and Sharon walked between buildings and down a short hall where a door opened into the altar end of the worship space. Row after row of mahogany-stained pews with burgundy cushions fanned out before them in three sections. More pews filled the back balcony. Adelia imagined them all filled with proud parents and brothers and sisters during graduation ceremonies.

The sun was high enough to give a nice light to the seven stained glass windows on either side. Some had Bible scenes. Some verses. A few were dedicated to individuals or groups. One on the south side recorded names of the committee that spearheaded the building of the new sanctuary. The name John Noble Maxwell was familiar.

"This building is quite different from the original. Even the one in between," Sharon said. "I'll show you a sketch of the first structure when we get back to the office."

"I understand Swann Marks was the organist here for many years," said Adelia, as they walked for a moment in the foyer. "Played for the memorial service after Franklin Roosevelt's death."

"She was also the secretary at the school, I believe," said Sharon.

"Indeed she was. A student I met in town said she was wonderful. Knew everyone and everything," said Adelia. "I'm sorry I can't talk with her. She died a few years ago in Richmond."

"Let me show you something," Sharon said as they headed back toward the communion rail. "We have an electric organ now, but look at this." She opened a door revealing row upon row of original organ pipes.

"Oh," Adelia gasped appreciatively at the banks of blue. "It's a shame so many churches have gone to electric instruments. I love the old organ sound from the beautiful pipes, especially horizontal trumpets."

She remembered her first trumpet enchamade, seen in a Northeastern Oklahoma church while she wrote an article on the reconditioning of the pipes and keyboard. She recalled the scattered pipe locations and hidden keyboards of the cathedral in Canterbury, England and contrasted them in her mind with the screened pipes and prominent four-level keyboard of the organ at her alma mater. Every student there remembered two things, the Ka-Rip spirit chant and the playing of 'Trumpet Voluntary' at all official ceremonies. Many used the early eighteenth century piece in their weddings.

Back in the church office, Sharon brought out a sheet of heavy paper with a pencil sketch of a small wooden church. It had two lancet doors in front and was crowned by a rectangular, louvered steeple topped by a tented roof and short mast.

"This must be what it was like near the turn of the century, maybe a little later," Adelia said. "I'll have to look it up at the library. And, I'll call to see what Sheila can tell me."

Chapter 18

Adelia was surprised to see all the lights on as she drove up Reservoir Street, arriving home after eleven from her afternoon-evening shift at Kinko's in Charlottesville. By this hour, everything was usually quite, with the twenty-something guys in from their jobs at the pizza place and John and Tilley and their guests upstairs or in the pool room.

"Oh, it's Lonnie's birthday party," she remembered as her car rolled to a stop in the back parking lot. Lonnie was one of the two partners who owned the complex and took advantage of that to throw quite a bash for his fortieth.

Adelia thought about trying to enter by the Montessori wing or the front porch on the northwest corner. But those doors were locked during public functions. She had to come through the back door and down the hall through the zigzag to the grand staircase. She was under-dressed for the occasion, clothed efficiently for seven hours on her feet and squatting to clear copy jams.

A woman in gold lamé top and long black skirt stood at the foyer end of the back hall. At least the gentleman in the conversation had shed his suit coat. Another couple sat on the lower stairs, she in bright red silk shirt and black palazzo pants and he in khakis and a dark blue cotton sweater with the sleeves pushed up. Many more guests moved back and forth between the ballroom and entrance hall.

"Excuse me," Adelia said, walking through quickly and ducking under the rope stretched across the stairs just before the landing. She wondered at the flimsy clothesline barrier and whether anyone would bother to read the attached sign, "Please do not proceed further."

Mollie was glad to see Adelia, since she was bothered by strange situations without her mom around. However, the cocker should be growing accustomed to the merriment after experiencing a high school prom, the Fishburne Military School Cotillion, and a wedding reception.

Adelia missed them all since she worked across the mountain on the weekends. She once retrieved a piece of wedding cake from a box in the stainless steel jumble of the yet uncleaned catering prep room. Hmmmm! It was so hard to get that white cake with the real creamy sweet icing. Mollie enjoyed her small portion almost as much as the pizza that afternoon.

This night, the cocker wagged an enthusiastic greeting—with what little tail she had—but gave a warning whine after being in for ten hours. Adelia clicked on the leash and took her down the back stairs and out the front porch on the end. They walked across the space in front of the flagpole terrace and sat on the granite step so Adelia could relax from a hectic day at work while soaking up some of the party atmosphere.

The band quit promptly at midnight. However, a number of guests were still in the entrance hall when Adelia and Mollie went up the porte-cochere steps. Adelia was too tired to wait them out, and Mollie was ready for her late night snack. Guests smiled at the two of them, and one lady bent down to pet Mollie. Her companion reached over to straighten her glass so the red wine would not spill on her beaded white dress, or on the dog.

Good save, thought Adelia.

***

Walking by the arched office window the next morning, Adelia spied an edge of paper peeking out from under the closed screen. Her curiosity won out and she pulled it forward. It was an auction advertisement from January 5, 1995.

"In the Heart of the Shenandoah Valley!" boasted the headline.

24.1 Acres of Multi-Family Residential Land in 3 Parcels and Fairfax Hall Boarding School Facility in 3 Grand Historic Buildings. Prime for Development and Redevelopment in the Heart of Waynesboro, Virginia.
(Picture)
"Will All Sell at Absolute AUCTION
Thursday, January 12th - 10:30 a.m.
For More Information
Call Agents BLAND LAND CO. . . .

Adelia recalled a similar availability-to-buy flyer from Barnwell and Jones dated March, 1993. It offered a site development plan "encompassing the construction of townhouse and single family units while contemplating elderly congregate care, maintaining the integrity of the core buildings and grounds." The Gates-Nash family partnership that owned the property wanted eight-hundred ninety-five thousand dollars.

Her research showed an offer of eight hundred thousand made earlier by the Department of Corrections. It was rejected at that time by the partnership which insisted on one million.

At auction almost two years later, Adelia's landlords, Tony and Lonnie, bought the 14.7-acre largest parcel, with the buildings, for one hundred seventy-five thousand. Katherine and Pat paid ten thousand dollars for each of the 5.85 front-lawn acres. And a developer bought the 3.5 acres across the road for seventeen-thousand, two-hundred an acre. A total of under three-hundred thousand dollars.

"Hi, Adelia. There's another piece in here," John said, walking into the office and opening a cabinet door.

The booklet read "Paragon Publications Real Estate Flyer, March 9-22, 1995. Vol. 1 No. 1". On the front was a picture of the building with "For Sale – Fairfax Hall – For Lease. A Unique Landmark Development Opportunity."

"Nice words, no results," John said. "My mom goes into the ballroom every morning and prays that it becomes a nursing home. A church group wanted to make it into a finishing school for high school graduates who want to go to college. One group wanted a hotel. The city is talking about rebuilding the outdoor pool into a regional storm water retention pond."

He continued reciting the prospective buyers. "Some people who want to make it an Oxford-type Korean College came back for a second visit last week. Maybe they will be the ones."

Adelia's heart skipped a beat. Her oral lease agreement went from month to month. There weren't too many places where she could afford to live in the area. And, Mollie was a complicating factor.

John seemed to sense her horror. "I wouldn't worry too much. People just don't realize what it will take to renovate it. They had an estimate in 1989 for eight-hundred-fifteen thousand."

Adelia had thought about this. "They'd have to put in at least one elevator and probably two. And there's a lot of miscellaneous work to do. I'd say more like three or four million. Still, this brochure must have attracted some attention."

> The Fairfax Hall site, comprising
> 15 acres, offers a flexible approach to
> development, or alternatively, restoration
> and refurbishing of the certified historic
> main structures, reviving the ambiance
> which sets Fairfax Hall and its grounds apart. . . .
>
> The main building, a sprinklered structure
> of over 60,000 square feet constructed in
> the late 1800s is particularly charming and
> unique, making a definite statement.

"Then there's this sentence," chuckled John. "The characteristic qualities of Fairfax Hall are best experienced through inspection."

* * *

The next morning, Adelia was washing dishes when she decided to call Allen at Lake Ann Camp in Michigan. She was not keen on moving back north, and she had no reason to think there was a job there. But the impulse to call was very strong.

Mollie came over to comfort her mom who was crying minutes after hanging up the phone. "It's okay little girl," Adelia said. "I just can't believe it. There may be a position there."

Nine whirlwind days later she accepted the job as development assistant and had five days to pack, find a moving company, and hope that David, her new boss, could find her an apartment in Allegan that accepted dogs.

Daley agreed to supervise the loading of the moving van. Adelia got in two short research sessions at the library. Even Mollie wagged her tail at an unknown new adventure.

As Adelia drove down the front driveway, she thought, "I never did get in to see the rooms of the Montessori school." The loss was minor. Her last research revealed that the north perpendicular was built decades after the wedding.

The package arrived by UPS at her office in Michigan just before Adelia left for the gym. It was the size of a small box of spaghetti, as heavy but not as noisy. The return address read, "Daly, 549 Cranapple Street, Waynesboro, Virginia, 22980." Adelia tore off the brown paper to find a note inside atop another wrapping marked with her former location and a return address from Dillwyn, Virginia.

"Dear, Adelia," the note read. "Your friend, the secretary at First Baptist Church, gave me your address. This came for you a couple of weeks ago.

"Hope your job is great, but how do you stand the winters in Michigan? Joy and Bo miss your pizza and cookies and Mollie. George is still working with John on Tony's construction crew. And we are happy to be in a regular house now. Did you ever find out any more about the locket? Write me a few lines when you get the time. Fondly, Daly."

Adelia carefully unwrapped the enclosed package, taking care to preserve the address. Inside, on top of a fettuccine box—Didn't miss that by much, she thought.—was a folded slip of paper and a small newspaper clipping.

"Dear Adelia," the note read. "I hope this gets to you all right. I am sorry to say Gerald died last month. He never got his strength back after the pneumonia. However, we enjoyed talking about Fairfax Hall and the locket until the end.

"A few months ago, as we were going through some of his things, we came across this. Gerald said it was passed down to him by his father who got it from his father. He thought you should have it. He didn't say why, just that I should send it to you. By the way, did you ever find out anything more about the locket? I feel sure you would have written if you did. Send me a few lines when you have the time. Sincerely, Lisa."

Adelia wiped away a tear as she opened the box and unrolled the object from several sheets of tissue paper. It was a small hammer with a wooden handle rubbed smooth with much use. As she picked up the tissue paper and box to read the note again, Adelia spied the newspaper clipping. It was an obituary for Gerald Montague Payne III.

Chapter 19

Adelia knew the building had sold and was undergoing extensive renovation. The First Baptist Church secretary sent her a clipping from the *News-Virginian* last fall. A local developer, enlisting help from a group in Boston, partnered with the Virginia Housing Development Authority to build apartments for low-income elderly.

However, she could not believe the sight before her. Three trucks topped with ladders, several port-a-potties, collapsed orange-net fencing, and piles of shingles and long boards filled the top edge of the lawn, stretching down from the flagpole terrace.

Large sections of unstained shingles were blotches on the exterior walls. Suddenly Adelia knew what the other large mass of materials was along the driveway—the lower section of the cupola. Only a few new posts stood on top of the building now. A construction trailer sat beside the rear porch of the dining hall.

Adelia was traveling through Waynesboro on her way to Charlottesville on a traditional every-two-or-three-years-journey to Jefferson Country. It had been this way since 1976 when she first fell in love with Monticello and the University of Virginia. Without her "fix," Adelia had withdrawal symptoms of mild depression.

As she walked through the porte-cochere, she noted repairs to the piers which held the columnettes. Although John told her once that squirrels liked to nibble on the painted bricks, she assumed the damage was caused by cars backing into them. The level of noise from inside the main building was well above the decibels of Lonnie's birthday band.

Entering the front door, she saw a man in jeans and gray T-shirt carrying a long two-by-four on his shoulder. "Hi there. Can I help you?" he said.

Adelia thought he would make her don a construction hat, based on her quick surveillance of the lobby. "Hi, I'm Adelia. I used to live here, and I'm researching a book about this site. Is there someone I can talk to about what's going on?"

"Sure. Let me get Peter." He continued on his way toward the dining hall. Another man emerged a few minutes later.

"Hi, Adelia. I'm Peter. I understand you're interested in what we're doing here."

"Yes, thank you. I knew the building was being renovated, but this—"

"We've pretty much finished gutting it and doing critical restructuring," Peter said. "Since it's a national historic site, the lobby and the dining room will be restored about the same."

Adelia was glad he paused for a breath so she could begin to take it all in.

"That includes repairing and refinishing this original tongue and groove pine and hardwood strip flooring." The technical jargon rolled off his tongue. "We're adding support to all the columns here, and we are replacing one, as you can see here, that was taken out earlier." He shook his head and muttered something about damage caused to the parlor.

"But the rest of the interior areas will be very different. Would you like to take a tour?"

"Sure, that would be super." Adelia said a silent prayer of thanks for her good fortune.

"Let's go down this way first," he pointed out the front door, allowing Adelia time to put her things in front of the office grille. "I have to check on some work in the basement." As they went, Peter explained that the porch and steps would be replaced, right down to the painted wood treads and risers and two cement steps at the bottom.

A few feet after entering the wide open space once occupied by the north door and side windows, Adelia saw several workmen smoothing a large expanse of glittering gray cement where the two classrooms had been. Walls, once covered in neglected blackboards, were absent from the enclosure of pillars.

"This used to be a wood floor on joists," Peter said. "We hauled in tons of gravel to form the base for this. It wasn't until we started clearing the building that we discovered all kinds of structural flaws," he explained with an incredulous shake of this head.

"The floors on this end have pancaked," he continued, obviously well-versed in the work. "See that beam where the board just sticks out to the left?" He pointed up to the northwest corner through the open area where the second floor would have been.

Adelia nodded although she wasn't sure what she was supposed to appreciate.

"When they put on the third floor, they just nailed the new floor braces on without adding other support. It's amazing it hasn't collapsed.

"Over here is where one of the elevators will be" He pointed to a round hole, about ten inches across, in the area of the former dumb waiter. We had to drill down thirty-six feet for the box to contain the elevator jam."

Adelia was speechless, unable to wrap her mind around that. Everything about the building always pointed upward.

They went down the perpendicular hall where Peter pointed out the spider glass of the old post office room. "We're going to keep as many of these features as we can. What's behind them, of course, will be very different."

On the other side of the hall, with no walls, Adelia spied the four steps down from the level on the right to that on the left. "What's this?" she asked.

"We're not sure why there's a difference?" he said, leading her down the steep and tiny steps. "We know that this wing was added on some time after the hotel was built. You can see where the buildings were joined here. And, we know there was a fire at one time. See the burn marks on the timbers?" Adelia nodded.

Climbing the steps at the end of the hall, they went through the Montessori entrance, where Adelia was shocked by the cement block structure on the left. "That's for the new enclosed stairway," Peter explained "It will be covered in wood shake to match the rest of the exterior.

"Remember the steps down here?" He pointed beside the new tower. "We had to take them out, which turned out to be very difficult. They were built so well we brought in a bulldozer to crush them into pieces and lift them out."

As they walked to the middle wing, Adelia found two major structures missing, the large wooden staircase to the second floor and the long low building between the wings. "That deck should never have been put in," Peter said, responding to her questions. "And someone wanted the big tank that used to be over there to supply water to the sprinkler system.

"He brought over a front end loader to get it. But the tank was so heavy that it kept tilting the loader over. It was something to watch," he smiled. "It took three complicated maneuvers and most of the morning to get the tank onto the flatbed truck."

Inside the kitchen hallway, most of the walls were gone, although the back stairway into John and Tilley's wing was still there. "We'll be taking those stairs out soon," Peter said. "That's where the control panel for the electrical and sprinkler systems will be."

As they passed through the zigzag and reached the end of the back passage, Peter stopped suddenly. "This was the other big surprise." He pointed across the hall to the open floor space.

"We knew from the first inspection that the floors on this end sloped." Adelia nodded and explained her own discovery while living on the second floor.

"We didn't know why until we got under this floor. For one thing the footings were misplaced and not large enough," he explained. "Again, it's the addition of the third floor problem, although the structure probably would have survived. Except. . . ."

The pause was breathtaking. Adelia could see he took great pleasure in it.

"Except, right about here, we found the real reason." He pointed to a space near the previous inside wall of the parlor. "In the original construction, there was a twenty-five-foot support joist made of three big timbers. All three had knotholes at the same place. Eventually the weight caused them to break." The accompanying look reflected more strange coincidence, this time, than incredulity.

"We had to lift up three-hundred-and-fifty tons on this corner and put a six-thousand-ton beam in place."

"Wow," Adelia said appreciatively.

"The other elevator will be right here," Peter pointed to the parlor area. "There will also be space for residents' mailboxes. And we'll build restrooms here. The ladies' will include the fireplace, but not as a working element."

They walked quickly through the dining room where Peter explained the limited changes and onto the rear porch where stood a new wooden staircase. "We had to add another egress from the upper floors on this end," he explained. "This will be blocked off from the dining room and other porch. The local developer kept the rights to the kitchen, dining hall, and porch to rent out for community events."

He explained that residents would have a small dining room in the former pool room area when they need extra room for serving guests, but no cooking facilities. Of fifty-four rental units, there would be one two-bedroom apartment, one efficiency, and fifty-two one-bedrooms with baths and sitting areas.

"I guess you have quite a soundproofing job to do," Adelia said. "I shouldn't think seniors will want to put up with a lot of noise from big events." The comment got no response.

"At least they have lots of space to walk and enjoy the trees and flowers and things." She tried again.

"Actually not," Peter said. "The parcel includes only a little land around the building. All of it on the north side will be used for a residents parking lot. The two sellers still own the land by the swimming pool and all the structures and land in the back. And the pasture is privately owned."

How strange, thought Adelia as they started to climb the main staircase to the second floor. Peter pointed out holes in the overhead beam where gingerbread would be reattached.

Although the linoleum remained largely undisturbed, wires pierced further-worn walls and dangled from the ceiling. Odd remains and new pieces of plumbing were spaced through the support columns and now-exposed brick fireplaces. Long boards lay on the floor, doors balanced against fireplaces, and old window casements flanked outer wall structures. Where the studs were uncovered, Adelia saw diagonal boards running between them.

"You'll notice there is no plywood," Peter followed her gaze. "Very wide boards, much wider than you could find today. And look at the studs. Much bigger." Adelia gauged them at about one-and-a-half inches compared to the three-quarters-inch modern.

"They're all hand cut with saws, hatchets and chisels," Peter added, leading Adelia to the south end. "We had to reconfigure the apartments here because of this special arched-beam construction for the dining hall." He pointed to peaks rising through the floor joists. The trusses, he explained, are composite wood and steel.

"Some of the beams in other areas were rotted through from water damage and crumbled like potting soil" he continued. "Where we can, we're placing plywood and metal sheets around the old beams, held together with bolts, to strengthen them. And we have to replace the flooring on the upper floor because the beams were improperly sized during the original construction."

They walked to the north end for a better view of the poor construction Peter mentioned earlier. "Over to the right there," he pointed near the offending corner structure, "we found this big hole in the wall, boarded up and plastered over. Sloppily, I might add."

Adelia felt a sudden chill. "I don't know," he continued. "Maybe it was originally access to the old roof before the third floor was put in.

"To correct the pancaking on this end, we're having to build the floor—the concrete slab you saw in the basement," he reminded. "Then the walls, the floor, the walls, etc.—all the way through the third floor. Then there's the attic."

"The attic can use a lot of work," said Adelia, noting the cracks she had seen in the roof and the horrible shape of the missing cupola.

"Oh, the cupola is being rebuilt to original specs as required," said Peter.

"We're putting on a new roof of fiberglass shingles to replace the asphalt ones. And we are cleaning out a lot of debris between the ceiling joists of the third floor." He shook his head at the state of things.

"We're repairing the rock and stone foundation; the mortar has deteriorated to the point of collapse due to water damage. We're putting a new rubber roof on top of the porte-cochere and just a million other little things it seems," Peter said.

"But it's really going to be nice," he said proudly. "Another three to five years and it would have been beyond salvaging, maybe parts actually falling down.

"Be careful as you come down these," Peter said as he led her down the back stairs.

Adelia finally saw the auditorium—mostly gutted. The ceiling had exposed beams trimmed in dark stained wood. On the east end a polished ledge protruded.

"At some time, the stage was walled off," Peter said, "but we're leaving the proscenium as a nice little feature in this apartment."

They walked back to the office hall and stopped at the reception desk where Adelia retrieved her camera case and keys.

"Well, this is quite a job," she said.

"Almost totally redoing fifty-five thousand square feet," Peter said with a big grin.

"You must have . . . I mean, tearing it all apart like this, you must have found some interesting things," Adelia said. "No ghosts, I guess."

"No, no ghosts or any signs of tools moved during the night," Peter smiled. "Just some objects. Mercury dimes under baseboards, a newspaper from 1939, a medicine bottle."

He paused in his list to give details. "It was really quite pretty. Rectangular with a heavy neck and remains of a stopper. The label said pentacine, I think it was. For headaches. And we found one for stomach trouble.

"And on the second floor. . . . It was near that hole I told you about," he said. "We found a chisel stuck between a beam and a cross piece. It was in so tight we had to leave it. The interesting thing was that there was a locket on the chisel, hanging from a silver chain."

Adelia nearly fainted. Peter did not notice, enjoying the telling of another discovery.

"Inside was a lock of hair and a small piece of paper folded several times," he said. "The developer put the locket in a box of things for display in the lobby later. But I have a copy of the paper right here. Kind of strange," he said, opening one of the counter drawers.

Somehow Adelia focused on the words.

> *To my dearest Old Pills. On our*
> *wedding day, we shall add a lock of your*
> *own. And, some day when we are old*
> *and gray, let us have these little tokens*
> *of our young selves and know then how*
> *precious memories will always linger.*
>   *Love, Reggie.*

About the Author

Elizabeth Tidwell has been a professional writer for over thirty years, primarily as a journalist and public relations specialist and consultant. *Memories Will Always Linger*, her first novel, combines a love of history with skills of research, interviewing, observation and telling. She finally found the right site for a mystery novel and has great acquaintance with it, having lived in Fairfax Hall for over a year. The story developed along the way as she did research about the site and surrounding area.

She writes part-time at her home just south of Charlottesville, Virginia. Most days, and many evenings, you will find her working for the University of Virginia or giving tours of Thomas Jefferson's home, Monticello.

Her next novel may take her to Al Capone's Northern Michigan retreat or somewhere along the Lewis and Clark Trail, if she can just find the right site.

Printed in the United States
31454LVS00002B/82-225